In Other Words

In Other Words
New Writing by Indian Women

edited by

URVASHI BUTALIA & RITU MENON

Introduction by Roshni Rustomji-Kerns

Westview Press
BOULDER • SAN FRANCISCO • OXFORD

All rights reserved. No part of this publication may be reproduced or transmitted in any form or by any means, electronic or mechanical, including photocopy, recording, or any information storage and retrieval system, without permission in writing from the publisher.

Copyright © 1994 by Kali for Women

Published in 1994 in the United States of America by Westview Press, Inc., 5500 Central Avenue, Boulder, Colorado 80301-2877

First published in 1992 in India by Kali for Women, A 36 Gulmohar Park, New Delhi 110 049

Library of Congress Cataloging-in-Publication Data
In other words : new writing by Indian women / edited by Urvashi
  Butalia and Ritu Menon.
    p. cm.
  ISBN 0-8133-2214-6 — ISBN 0-8133-2172-7 (pbk.)
  1. Short stories, Indic (English)—Women authors.   2. Indic
fiction—20th century.   I. Butalia, Urvashi.   II. Menon, Ritu.
PR9494.5.W66I6 1994
823'.01089287—dc20   94-1943
                                                                    CIP

Printed and bound in the United States of America

The paper used in this publication meets the requirements of the American National Standard for Permanence of Paper for Printed Library Materials Z39.48-1984.

10   9   8   7   6   5   4   3   2   1

Acknowledgement

A Government of India Undertaking first appeared in *Imprint* (1984); *Dooz, Charu and the Establishment*, in *Indian Horizons* No. 2 (1982); *The Smothering*, in *Debonair* (1989); *The Remains of the Feast*, as *Forbidden Fruit*, in *Debonair* (1990); *The Tamarind Tree Murder*, in *London Magazine* (1992); *Sara*, in *Lilies that Fester*, Writers Workshop (1988).

Contents

Introduction ix
  Roshni Rustomji-Kerns
Glossary xxv

A Government of India Undertaking 1
  Manjula Padmanabhan
No Letter from Mother 25
  Vishwapriya L. Iyengar
Twilight 33
  Manju Kak
Dooz, Charu and the Establishment 40
  Subhadra Sen Gupta
Portrait of a Childhood 49
  Shama Futehally
Thanks, anyway 58
  Achla Bansal
The Smothering 66
  Ritu Bhatia
Rites of Passage 80
  Bulbul Sharma
Dying Like Flies 92
  Ruchira Mukerjee

The Manuscript 107
  Deep Bedi

The Remains of the Feast 136
  Githa Hariharan

Mallika Farida 146
  Shalini Saran

The Tamarind Tree Murder 156
  Urmila Banerjee

Sara 170
  Manorama Mathai

  Notes on Authors 193

Introduction

ROSHNI RUSTOMJI-KERNS

I have tried to tell of a life lived in limbo ... but perhaps I was only telling of myself and did not, as I fancied, step through the mirror.

—Manorama Mathai, *Sara*

There has not been a woman who did not take the opportunity to contemplate her image reflected in the mirrors that fate has put before her. When the crystal of the waters becomes turbid and the eyes of the man in love close and the litany of the poets is exhausted ... there is still another recourse: to construct her self-image, a self-portrait, to draft her defense, to exhibit the proof of discharge, to draft her will for posterity (in order to give it what she had, but, most of all, to certify what she lacked), to evoke her life.

—Rosario Castellanos, *Mujer que sabe Latin*

THE LITERATURE OF India is not a homogenized body of works. Indian women's writings do not emerge out of one tradition of literature nor do they reflect one common vision of a shared sociopolitical history.

Instead, the background of literatures and history against and into which Indian women write their stories is highly complex and diverse. *In Other Words* illustrates the multiplicity and range of Indian women writers.

It is generally believed that silence and quiet acceptance have traditionally been expected from the women of India. But the images of women protagonists in Indian literature have not always been of passive, quiet women. There are a number of memorable women in Indian literature who are magnificently adept at using words. Portraits of women who lead very different lives, who have their own unique visions and ideas, and who are not afraid to use their words and actions to manipulate the world they live in populate Indian literature, both oral and written, from the earliest times to the present. For example, one can point to several women (mortal and immortal) in the hymns of the Rig Vedas (ca. 1200–900 BCE) who speak up about their ideas, desires, and complaints in dialogues, conversations, and narratives that deal mainly with their relationships with men.

The voices of the women of the Rig Vedic hymns are continued and amplified in the *itihasa* (epic) tradition, which began around 900 BCE with the *Mahabharata*. The *Mahabharata* tells of the great war between two sets of cousins and contains an enormous cast of female and male characters: mortals, immortals, and semi-mortals. It weaves narratives within narratives and legends and mythology within the larger framework of the main story. Among the many women who inhabit the world of the *Mahabharata* are three very important women who are not afraid to use language to gain their ends. The main female protagonist, Draupadi, queen and wife of the five Pandavas, does not quietly lament her fate when one of her husbands gambles her away in a game he is compelled to play with his enemy. She is loud in her anger and forces a debate on the legality of her husband's right to use her as a wager in his game. She makes her outrage heard even in the divine realm. The legendary figure of Shakuntala bargains with the king who tries to seduce her. Later she presents her case in the king's court after he has disregarded the bargain he had agreed upon and has abandoned her and their son. Savitri, another woman from one of the many legends in the epic, talks Death into giving back her husband through persuasion and verbal trickery.

In the romance-epic the *Ramayana*, Sita is the heroine. The exile of her husband, Prince Rama, due to the machinations and verbal skills of two women; the abduction of Sita while in exile with her husband; and the quest for Sita and the battle to regain her form the core of this long poetic narrative. Again, Sita is not quietly submissive, as some people wish to portray her. She speaks up for her right to go into exile with her husband. And later, when abducted by Ravana, she does not hesitate to protect herself with fearless words.

The unjustly accused and executed hero of the Tamil epic *Shilappadikaram* (The Ankle Bracelet) (third century CE) is avenged by his wife, Kannagi. Kannagi, who has appeared in the narrative as the traditional quiet, gentle, long-suffering wife, turns into a furious woman. She rushes through the city proclaiming her grief and crying against the injustice meted out to her husband and herself. She barges into the palace and personally accuses the king. She proves her husband's innocence, narrates stories about women who prevailed over injustice, and then curses the city clearly and loudly.

These images and voices of women in early Indian literature were certainly created for public display by male artists. One can speculate about the reasons for the appearance of these portraits in a literature written by men. Beyond the discussion of the possible rights and equality enjoyed by Indian women in early Indian societies and the existence of matriarchal societies in India, one can explore the portrayal of these women protagonists as being based upon the realities of oral literature. The strong presence of Indian women as creators and performers—within the family and the larger community—of family histories, folk songs, religious stories, devotional songs, mythological and legendary narratives, and of oral literature in general has always been acknowledged. The voices of these women may be partially responsible for the verbal strength of some of the women protagonists in the ancient and classical hymns, epics, dramas, and poetry.

Women protagonists in classical Indian literature were not only portrayed as speakers of great talent but were also often portrayed as writers of commendable skill. In some of the classical Sanskrit dramas of the early centuries of the Common Era, we are presented with queens, women dwellers of ashrams, Buddhist nuns, and brilliant courtesans who read, write, and debate with grace, wit, and an enviable command over the language. There is also a magnificent statue from Khajuraho (tenth century CE) of a woman writing. She is adorned with jewelry, her clothes traced lightly around her body, her face bent over the tablet in her left hand and the writing stylus in her right hand, her entire being concentrated upon her writing.

We not only hear about and see portraits of women writers in early Indian literature and art, we also know of women writers of early classical and medieval literature. One needs only to glance through the Table of Contents of the two-volume anthology *Women Writing in India*[1] to become aware of the long and continuous history of Indian women writers as well as the range and variety of literature they have produced.

Works by Buddhist nuns (sixth century BCE) are sometimes discussed as the earliest women's writings that have survived in India. But in the Rig Vedas, Hymn 10.40 to the Ashvins (the twin horsemen and healers, sons of the Sun) has traditionally been attributed to Ghosha, who refers to herself in the hymn as "the daughter of a king." Anthologies of the highly elaborate court poetry (early centuries of the Common Era) include verses by women poets such as

Vidya and Bhavaka. The medieval *Bhakti* (devotion) tradition of poet-saints who rejected established hierarchies and orthodoxy has often been traced to the Tamil woman poet Karraikal Ammaiyar (eighth century CE). The songs of many famous women poet-saints, such as Meera and Lalleshwari, are revered and sung to this day.

As we read, discuss, and evaluate the impressive corpus of works by Indian women writers, we need to remember that this literature has been created and has survived against great odds. Women have always had to overcome special problems in order to write and to be read. Economical problems, problems of education, problems of finding time and space to write, and the struggle against prejudice and fear constantly challenge women who write. But women have not been easily persuaded away from creating literature. They have insisted on writing whenever and wherever they have discovered an opportunity. The seemingly insurmountable problem in the history of women's literature has been the problem of reaching an audience—of being published, read, and accepted seriously as writers. Even today, the extensive and excellent body of literature by Indian women, which is gradually being accepted in India as an integral and important part of Indian literature, is barely acknowledged outside of India. For example, women's groups in the United States are willing to look at Indian women's lives through the disciplines of anthropology and the social sciences, but seldom do they listen to the voices of Indian women writers.

It is my hope that the publication and reprinting of anthologies such as *In Other Words* will make the writings of Indian women more accessible to Western audiences.

The writers represented in this volume emerge from a distinct political and literary history. Their immediate ancestresses are the women writers of the second part of the nineteenth and the early part of the twentieth century. Through their writings and political activities, Indian women of that period documented as well as participated in their country's struggle for socioeconomic reform and for independence from British rule. Names of important Indian women writers such as Pandita Ramabai Saraswati, Ramabai Ranade, Sarojini Naidu, Rokeya Sakhawet Hossain, and Mahadevi Varma can be read against the background of the sociopolitical movements of this period of Indian history. One could begin this period with the militant uprisings of 1857–1858 against the British, then move to the inauguration of the Indian National Congress in 1885, the founding of the Muslims League in 1906, Gandhi's first nationwide Civil Disobedience movement in 1940, the "Quit India" movement beginning in 1942, the independence and partition of India in 1947, the coming into effect of the Constitution of India in 1950, the first General Election in 1952, and end with the election of Indira Gandhi in 1966 and her assassination in 1984. If the writers mentioned at the beginning of this paragraph were the only women writers of those times, it would be an impressive list. But this is a partial list of the important women writers from those years. In the 1930s, when a number of writers, most of them involved with socialist causes and politics, began forming Progressive Writers Associations, women such as Kamaladevi Chattopadhyay, Ismat Chugtai, Rasheed Jehan, and Sarojini Naidu became involved in the organization and the ongoing work of these groups. The terrible violence, especially against women and children, during and after the 1947 partition of India was lamented, documented, and fiercely denounced in the poetry, short stories, novels, and essays of women such as Amrita Pritam, Ismat Chugtai, Attia Hosain, and Suraiya Qasim.

The writers of *In Other Words*, most of whom were born after 1947, have inherited the political-literary history of the century that led to the independence of India, and they have grown up as women and writers experiencing the betrayal of the political and socioeconomic goals and dreams of those who had struggled for independence and reform.

Thirty-seven years after independence, the New Delhi–based journal about women and society *Manushi* published a collection of articles that had appeared in the journal from 1979 to 1983. The collection is titled *In Search of Answers: Indian Women's Voices from Manushi*.[2] In her introduction, Madhu Kishwar repeatedly emphasizes the fact that the lives of the majority of Indian women (and the lives of the majority of Indian men) are spent struggling for the necessities of life. It is not a question of a room of her own; it is the basic question of food, water, fuel, and a roof for the woman as well as for her family. Kishwar points out that in spite of the belief among some urban Indians that Indian women won equality for themselves a long time ago, most Indian women face constant injustices and poverty. It is true that in 1930 the leaders of the Indian National Congress promised women equal political rights and a strong voice in independent India. And laws were passed after independence that in principle and on paper granted women equality and rights. It is also true that India has had a woman prime minister and that women appear in nearly every political and professional area. But too many women in India are still powerless to exercise their rights due to their economic and social conditions.

The reality of the status of women began to be questioned seriously by Indians in the 1970s when reports of physical, emotional, and mental violence against large numbers of women, even educated middle-class women, began to be publicized widely. The growing knowledge of married women being used as pawns and hostages in the escalating demands for larger dowries (illegal in India) and the maltreatment and even murder or forced suicide of women by their in-laws and husbands forced many Indians—women and men—to realize that women in India are still tragically too often subjected to the demands and cruelty of those who hold the power in the family. The 1974 publication of *Towards Equality: Report of the Committee on the Status of Women in India* documented the political and social inequalities faced by women. The findings of the committee and the rapidly increasing volume of reports on violence against women at all levels of society, within and outside their homes, led to the formation of numerous groups and organizations to discuss and actively deal with women's issues—issues that Indian women writers had never ceased to present in their works.

The maltreatment of women in the public and the private arenas as well as the fight against these injustices and abuses continue to be documented and narrated by Indian writers. While acknowledging and recording the victimization of women, many Indian women refuse to remain passive victims. The act of speaking up about abuse against women—in writing or in dramatic presentations on stage, movie screens, or street theatres—is the first step toward recording and publicizing the status of women. The documenting of injustices is an action that leads the way to acknowledging the critical need for important and basic political, social, and economic changes. This in turn often results in an active search and implementation of strategies for change. This process of documentation, the speaking out about everyday problems faced by Indian women, the unwillingness to remain victims, and the actions taken by some women are represented in a selection of letters to *Manushi* that have been published in *In Search of Answers*. One writer concludes, "Our struggle is going to be long and hard. ... And a feeling of aloneness in time of distress is terrible. We have to tell each other that we are not alone."[3] Another states, "I am the first woman in Karnataka to have filed a dowry case against my husband. ..."[4] In Meena Alexander's novel *Nampally Road*,[5] Mira Kannadical, a teacher of English literature in Hyderabad, and her mentor, Durgabai, help in the rescue of Rameeza. The story of Rameeza in this novel is based on an episode that occurred in Hyderabad in 1978. A poor woman who was visiting the town was dragged into the police station by a group of policemen who gang raped her and then threw her in jail. *Nampally Road* documents this case and ends with Rameeza freed from prison, a political uprising in town, and Mira's observation that "[Rameeza's] mouth was healing slowly." Her observation leaves the reader with a powerful image of a woman finding a voice to speak against and about injustice.

The political and social history discussed above puts the stories of *In Other Words* in context with regard to time and place. It is also important to explore the background of Indian traditions of literature and language that places the stories within the larger fabric of Indian literature.

There are certain human conditions, issues, and concerns that can be termed universal. But the voices raised to express and explore them remain individual to the writer and to her own historical and cultural world. Although all the stories in this book were written in English, and they were all, to some extent or another, influenced by the narrative traditions of English and other Western literatures, they are not "English" or "American" stories. Nor are they the products of an inaccessible "exotic" culture. They are stories from India written in English—a language that has become a part of the multi-linguistic life of India.

Since the earliest times of classical Indian literature (circa first century CE), Indian writers, musicians, and artists and their audiences and critics have discussed and debated the importance of *rasa*—the essential flavor, the mood, the emotions—and of *dhvani*—the suggestions, nuances, and overtones embedded in words, patterns of language, sounds, and colors as created and communicated through works of art. *Rasa* and *dhvani* still remain, consciously or subconsciously, overtly or subtly, the central elements in Indian discussions on the creation and enjoyment of art. For example, to really appreciate some of the stories, such as *A Government of India Undertaking, Rites of Passage,* and *The Tamarind Tree Murder,* in *In Other Words,* one needs to incorporate a discussion of the moods and emotions, the nuances of the language and narrative into the overall discussion of these works. The special lyrical language used to present a yearning for a lost time, a lost place, a lost beloved and the elegant use of language to explore abstract philosophical ideas and ideals and to juxtapose vibrant life with inescapable death are often discussed as the mark and the influence of Arabic and Farsi literature on Indian literature. *Mallika Farida* is a good example of the Islamic influence on Indian literature. The framework of the story, the characters, the stylized imagery used to describe Farida as she sits between two graves amidst silk and sequins, and her final words, "Mirza

Introduction xxi

Sahib ... there is no shrine as sacred as one's body..." give this narrative the sense of a beautifully executed Urdu poem.

The presence of the oral tradition of Indian literature can be heard in the voices of all the stories. Interestingly, twelve out of the fourteen stories are narrated in the first person. But it is not a uniform use of the first person narrative. The voices and the tones are as different and unique as they are in any good performance of oral literature for any audience. The voice of despair and the feeling of being "unmistakenly dead," as the author herself says, permeate *Portrait of a Childhood*. *Twilight* and *The Manuscript* turn into dramatic narratives as we hear the authors skillfully change the voices and points of view within their stories. Contemporary as *Dooz, Charu and the Establishment* is, it does not escape the age-old tone of a woman telling the story about her encounter with a beloved but difficult friend to a group of her friends. Manorama Mathai, in the best tradition of oral literature, speaks directly to us as she draws us into the narrative of her loveless life and her attempts to patch together the story of her grandmother Sara. In *Sara* and even in *The Smothering* one hears the sadness and the courage of countless folk songs sung throughout India by women, songs about the lives of women married into families and to husbands who betray them.

Many of the stories in this book are unexpected and startling. Not in the use of language, not in the styles and forms, not in the stories they tell, but in the central issue around which they build their narratives. The political and social milieu of these stories are those of the twentieth century. The sense of betrayal, of frustration and anger, if not explicitly present in all the stories, certainly lurks around the edges and between the lines of most of the stories. But the dominating obsession of many of the stories seems to be with the creation of a literary work. The art of the narrative, spoken and written, the attempt to compose the story itself, and the exploration of techniques to include the story guessed at within the story presented become the central issue. The whole question of women afraid of writing and of women writing not in their mother-tongue but in English is expressed in *No Letter from Mother*. The mother writes, "Please do not beg for anything, not even a letter from me. Appa writes good letters. ... I cannot write in English. Your teachers will make fun of my English so I will not write again to you. ... Don't ask me to write again." The struggle to tell one's own side of the story to oneself and to a larger audience can be seen in *Twilight* and *Sara*. In *The Manuscript* we hear two men talk to us about a woman who kept a diary about her rich and destructive in-laws. She wants to write a novel and has asked her husband for "a holiday from all of you. Give me a year, let me finish this book. I will become a hollow shell if I don't."

The women writers in this collection of short stories are building upon, sometimes circumventing, at other times extending the traditions and expectations of Indian literature and world literature written in

English. But in the end, they use their writings to contemplate on themselves and their characters as storytellers who belong to the tradition of Indian women protagonists and writers who have always told their stories in their own words.

Notes

1. *Women Writing in India*, edited by Susie Tharu and K. Lalita (New York: The Feminist Press, 1991 and 1993).

2. *In Search of Answers: Indian Women's Voices from Manushi*, edited by Madhu Kishwar and Ruth Vanita (London: Zed Books Ltd., 1984).

3. Ibid., p. 298.

4. Ibid., p. 299.

5. Meena Alexander, *Nampally Road* (San Francisco: Mercury House, 1991).

Glossary

aangan: courtyard
amma/appa: mother/father
ayah: maid
bahu: bride
banian: undershirt/vest
bas: enough
bhajans: religious songs
bhel-puri: savoury snack of west India
biryani: a pilaf of rice and meat
bondas: savoury snack made with potatoes and deep fried

chaat: spicy savoury
chaatwala: maker and seller of *chaat*
chappals: slippers
chillum: long-stemmed pipe
chowkidar: watchman/guard
dhaba: roadside eatery
dhobi: washerman
dhoti: loincloth
dosa: savoury snack of south India
dupatta: a veil draped across the bosom
dusserah: Hindu festival

FAO:	Food and Agriculture Organization of the United Nations
ganja:	marijuana
ghee:	clarified butter
GPO:	General Post Office
gulli-dunda:	a game played by striking two sticks, one long and one short
halvai:	sweetmeat vendor
havan:	ritual fire
Horlicks:	brand name of an energizing beverage
jalebis:	deep-fried sweetmeat, with syrup
janam:	birth
Kannada novels:	novels written in the language of the State of Karnataka (Kannada) in south India
kheer:	milk pudding
khus:	poppy seed
koftas:	savoury balls, deep-fried and curried
kookie:	hide-and-seek
kurta:	a long overshirt, worn traditionally by men and women
mangal grah:	inauspicious conjunction of the stars
mehndi:	henna
mulmul kurta:	muslin *kurta*
munshi:	accountant

neem datun:	twig of the *neem* tree, commonly used to clean one's mouth and teeth
neem tree:	a tree of the species *Azadirachta indica*
paan:	betel leaf
peepal tree:	a tree of the species *Ficus religiosa*, generally considered sacred
puja:	worship
puris:	deep-fried *rotis*
qawwals:	musicians who sing Sufi songs
raibahadur:	title conferred by the British for loyal service
rajnigandha:	tuberose
rotis:	flat bread made of unleavened wheat
salwar kameez:	an ensemble of loose pajamas caught at the ankle (*salwar*) and a long shirt (*kameez*)
sardar:	a Sikh
shraddha:	death ceremonies
sindoor:	vermilion powder, applied by married women to the parting of their hair
tonga:	horse-drawn carriage
vada:	deep-fried savoury snacks made of lentils
Valmiki:	author of the famous Indian epic *Ramayana*

A Government of India Undertaking...

MANJULA PADMANABHAN

ONE MORNING, I saw a balloon seller cross the street and vanish round a corner. I say "balloon seller", but he was more than that: against the bleakness of the city, its bone-grey buildings, its ragged people, its rubbish heaps and hidden rats, he had appeared as if from nowhere, a vision of youth and delight. High over his head swayed an immense bouquet of pink gas balloons, a hundred or more of them, alive, crowding together, bouncing apart, bright pink, bright with white specks. The balloon seller strode briskly along under their gay and thronging mass and, in a twinkling, had slipped from view, swallowed by the city.

So swiftly had he appeared and disappeared that I felt it my duty to run across the street and confront him again, if only to confirm the vision. But he was nowhere in sight. I wandered in and out of various little lanes and streetlets and caught nothing of him, no hint or sign that he had ever passed that way. It was on this pretext, looking for the balloon seller, that I entered a narrow gully with short squat buildings crowded one athwart the other and saw a sign which read: "Bureau of Reincarnation and Transmigration of Souls — A Government of India Undertaking". It was neatly hand-lettered in white paint on varnished wood, and contrasted strangely with the crumbling wall onto which it had been nailed.

I stood back to take a second look at the building, but no, it was just like all the rest to look at. Bleached, flaking paint, gaping doorway revealing a dark uninviting interior, a flight of worn wooden steps. There was a faint smell as of a bakery, or a urinal, perhaps. I stepped inside and noticed, once my eyes had adjusted to the gloom, an ancient chowkidar dozing on his wooden stool to the side of the door. Further in, a neat little peon sat at a small desk, staring with fixed purpose at its surface. It was covered with various objects: pencils, matchboxes, empty cigarette packets, an old glass ink-well and a paste-pot disfigured by successive encrustations of paste, and all of these arranged as for an obstacle course. I drew closer and saw that it was — for a shiny little cockroach was scrabbling about erratically, trying to reach the crumb of food dangled by the peon just beyond the reach of the insect's questing feelers. I saw too, that the creature's diligence would not be rewarded: down the leg of the desk, six of its brothers had been left to wriggle to their deaths skewered with government-issued straight pins. I watched in fascination, not daring to disturb the peon at his sport, to ask him where I should go and whom I should see in the Bureau of Reincarnation. But he anticipated me and said softly, not looking up from the desk, "Tea in

A Government of India Undertaking 3

fifteen minutes." I took this to mean that I should climb the flight of stairs, so I did.

Hardly had I reached the first floor, but I found I had joined a queue. That is, I arrived at the landing and was brought up short against a flesh-coloured room-divider which had a sign pasted on it which read: "Q this way -->". Further room-dividers had been laid out in a line, forming a sort of artificial corridor. I followed its length until, quite abruptly, I found I had entered a huge hall, with a vast mass of people apparently congealed along its floors and walls. Unaccountably, the building's internal dimensions had expanded and it was larger on the inside than its outside promised.

That queue was an amazing thing: not a group of individuals waiting patiently in line for something but an organic entity in itself. Physically, it was merely a more heroic version of the kind that one finds at the GPO during a sale of first-day issues. It looped backwards and forwards across that vast hall with its dingy marble chip tiling and dim, low-slung light bulbs. It passed over and under and right through itself so often that no one knew where it began or ended.

No one waiting in the queue (in my section of it, at least) could recollect having seen the waiting hall empty of people, nor was there anyone present who had been amongst the first to line up: everyone there had been waiting so long that he or she had lost all track of time and had settled into that vacuum of thought and action which is our only solace in such situations. It was in this time scale in a place where even the finest quartz watch was reduced to a useless curiosity by its sheer irrelevance, that the queue became as one animal, living, breathing and functioning as one organism and each of us in it making up its cell wall.

Nourishment in the form of regular cycles of tepid tea and stale chutney sandwiches passed through and reached every segment of the queue as efficiently and mysteriously as it appeared. We seemed to breathe in concert, each newcomer to the queue having to adjust himself/herself to the group rhythm — asthmatics had a bad time and smokers were not tolerated — until the walls seemed to move gently in and out with our respiration. The queue was constantly being depleted — as someone was finally ushered into the presence of an officer, registrar or file clerk — and constantly being replenished by newcomers to the queue and by former queue members rejoining the array in quest of yet another officer, registrar or file clerk. Since there was no distinct terminal point, each addition had to squeeze in as best he or she could, a few half-hearted grunts and tongue-clickings were raised in mild discontent, then everyone subsided once more into the vacant stupor of waiting.

For entertainment we had the endless forms, questionnaires and visiting slips to fill up, some of these transiting the length and breadth of the queue several times before being rescued by the defaulting peon and returned to the office of their origin. Sometimes we roused ourselves enough to sing bhajans and popular songs, sometimes there were a few listless bouts of gambling and once, someone who had brought a

A Government of India Undertaking   5

cassette recorder along, played a taping of last year's Test matches, and everyone cheered.

There were all kinds of people in that queue — you could tell at a glance from the myriad forms filled out in triplicate, the professions and personalities involved. The majority had come to check their claims for a better life the next time round: business magnates and thieves, they were each of them anxious to improve the fibre of their future lives. Others had come to look at the files of dear departed ones, to see if they could renew contact with them in the life to be; some had come to check on their antecedents, to see how well their current lives and companions matched their pasts; some had come belligerently, to demand enlightenment within the next three births or else, some had come out of idle curiosity and at least one pathetic individual I spoke to was there under the impression that he was in queue to buy tickets for *Deep Throat*. And finally, there must have been a few, like myself, who had come for dishonourable reasons but, naturally, I never actually spoke to any of the others.

Because of the irregular nature of my request, it took even more than the ordinary number of tea-and-sandwich cycles, false leads, wrong turnings along the queue and battles with insolent peons, coffee boys, receptionists and bureaucratic vagrants before I could approach my first bonafide officer — the Assistant Registrar of Files. He was a frail, desiccated, bright-eyed little man who smelt of clean old paper and wore rimless glasses. He sat behind an enormous desk generously littered with scraps of paper, forms, questionnaires and a few odd bus tickets. Holding down the papers were a dozen or so glass paperweights, the kind which look like gobs of some unspeakable mucus, quick-frozen and injected with air to produce five (sometimes four or less) bubbles inside, arranged in such a way as to keep the observer forever anxious to rearrange them more symmetrically. One of them, I noticed, a collector's item no doubt, had just one enormous tear-shaped bubble, and in it an ant had been trapped and preserved for posterity with a puzzled look on its face.

However, I had not come all that way merely to note down the details of interior decor in that musty little office. Leaning forward and putting as much earnestness as I could into my voice I said, "Sir, let me come straight to the point: ever since I saw the sign-board on the building, I have been possessed with the desire to" — I paused dramatically — "change my life." I had been looking at him directly when I said this last bit and was surprised and a little disappointed to see that the little man barely blinked. In fact he seemed on the verge of stifling a yawn, so I hurried on recklessly. "Oh, I realise this is an illegal request — even criminal you might say! But I've been waiting such a long time, and no one has so much as told me one way or another whether such a thing is possible at all." I tried to change my tack from wheedling to impatience: "I am at the end of my endurance. I must know what I need to know, even if my request is denied, but I must know. I am not going to leave this office until you can tell me what. . ."

But he stopped me by raising a delicate hand. For a moment I thought he was about to fob me off, as so many minions along the course of my ordeal had done, and I had my handful of tears collected and ready to throw in his face. But he pursed his lips a moment, then asked mildly, "But, have you filled out your death certificate?"

I was a little irritated. "Sir," I countered briskly, "surely it is obvious that I have not died. How, therefore, can I have filled out the death certificate?"

He had been waiting for this. "And if you have not died, my dear madam," he said, with the sort of patient, understanding smile that might be reserved for conversations with the mildly insane, "then how is it you want to change your life?"

"Ah, but that is just the point," I said, feeling great relief. This was the moment I had been waiting for, to unburden the true nature of my quest at the desk of a sympathetic officer. "You see, I am tired of my life and want to change it. But the thing is, I want to change it now. I do *not* want to commit suicide or go through all the mess of catching a disease or being murdered by jealous relatives or accidentally falling down mine shafts — besides, I took the trouble of bribing someone at the first floor Department of Mortality and she assured me that my dossier had not come up for review yet. As I need hardly remind you, the dossier must reach that office three full moons before a death is scheduled, in order that suitable allocations for the next life can be made." I paused for effect. "So what I thought was this: why not change it right now, in mid-life? I want to be rich. I want to be famous. I want to be absolutely indolent. And — I don't want to wait till my next life, I want it now."

He continued to be unimpressed. "Madam," he said, fidgeting daintily with his nose, "as you have stated, this is an illegal request?" He seemed to be asking for my opinion on the proposing of such requests.

"Well, yes," I said breezily, "but I don't care. I feel it can be quite simply arranged. In fact it is so simple that I'm absolutely certain other people must be doing this right now, that it must already be part of your system." I didn't want to come right out into the open and say that, since all government concerns are corrupt, this one must be equally so. I sincerely felt that it was just a question of understanding in what dimension it was corrupt and how the cogs of reincarnation had been realigned to suit the flavour of the corruption. "All that I'm asking is that I, with my lease on life, inhabit the body of someone else, preferably someone rich and comfortable, whose number has come up. Someone whose body is intact and in working condition but whose life has run its course. Don't you see how easily it could be done?"

A blink of light played about the bare rims of the Assistant Registrar's spectacles. "And your body, madam? What will happen to that?"

"Oh come now," I said, my confidence growing. "Surely it is of little concern — the rich person dies. I discard this body like a sweaty track suit and impinge upon the other one before its mechanism shuts down forever. Perhaps it could be one of those cases of coma in which a person who has been all but pronounced dead, miraculously revives. The only difference would be that instead of the original occupant returning to life there would be — me! So I don't care what you do with my body — keep it in coma perhaps? Loan it out to some soul kicking its heels about waiting to be reborn? To visiting extra-terrestrials?" I had spent my time in the queue fruitfully, I thought, and had actually advanced my scheme to include a scope of operations wider than my petty little life. I had the notion that, if I could only discover the actual process of transferring souls from corpse to new embryo, I could set up a sort of transmigrational banking system.

After all, I reasoned, this was just another government department: therefore there must be some sort of quota system, a waiting list of souls, a roster of lives waiting to be reborn. I imagined that there might even be a regular state-wide system of making allocations of how many lives could be legally issued per month or year or whatever — in fact I was amazed that the family planning programme had not set up permanent headquarters here. What I hoped to offer was in the way of a side attraction; a short trip to life while a soul awaited its legitimate birth. I did not feel any guilt at what I planned to do. If anything, I felt quite virtuous as I thought this might be the ideal way in which to bring home the point that it is really worthwhile to strive for release from the cycle of birth-death-rebirth. I had always felt that the system as I understood it was far too cumbersome: by the time a soul has done with being born, growing to maturity, struggling through childhood traumas and neuroses, the original purpose — that is of leaving the cycle entirely, by attaining enlightenment — is inevitably lost sight of. It seemed to be so unfair, so undemocratic. Under my system, a soul would be able to experience life without the confusing preamble of childhood and adolescence (especially adolescence) and perhaps, thereby, understand more clearly about the sorts of lives which lead to better results in the next. Maybe these visiting souls could even be trained to be a source of inspiration to their fellows doing time on earth, like freelancing messiahs, perhaps. All in all, I thought I had a fairly wonderful scheme worked out.

And still the Assistant Registrar was unimpressed! "Madam," he said, "do you think no one has considered this subject before?" He knew nothing, of course, of my grand vision, only of the basic request. He did not wait for my response. "So many people have approached us but we have always had to turn them down." He assumed a slightly professorial tone, leaning back and attempting to bring the tips of his fingers together in the classical posture of pedantry, but not succeeding very well because the arms of his chair were too wide apart for him to rest the elbows of his meagre little forelimbs. "Firstly, this is only the Department of Files: we make records, that is all. We have no direct jurisdiction over lives. Secondly. . . have you seen the files?"

For the first time, I looked up and around me, to take in the shelves which lined the room. I saw that the shelves were filled with files, then realised with a little start that the shelves were not exactly against the walls of the room, but that they were themselves the walls of the room, that behind them lay the possibility of further such glass-fronted filing cabinets; that the chamber in which they were housed could now be of entirely arbitrary proportions. I got up and went closer to one of the cabinets and saw that the files within were alphabetically marked — they were the same tatty old box files that one sees in bureaucratic concerns around the country, with papers spilling out, edges scuffed and dust-bitten, moulding under the excrement of generations of spiders. But the alphabets were not all in English. In fact some of them seemed barely human. "What are these files?" I asked, knowing that it was expected of me.

"All the births. All the deaths. We record everything," said that sage and prune-like man, with modest satisfaction. "Every birth, every death, every centimetre of every soul's journey along its personal path of release. Do you understand, madam, how many lives and deaths, progressions and regressions, we must be recording?"

"But. . ." I said, a vague sense of unease setting in, "I thought only people subscribing to a certain highly popular religion — only Hindus, in short — were eligible for rebirth?" I must admit that I had never really given the subject a thought until the moment of seeing the signboard. And then too, I had roughly generalised, thinking it unlikely that the government of one country would be entrusted with the reincarnation of the world's peoples. I just assumed therefore, that the Bureau's operations must be restricted to those people whose religion explicitly upheld such a belief.

"According to the propaganda, that is so," said the Assistant Registrar, "but in fact it is not of the least concern to the celestial office. And of course, you realise, madam, that I am not talking of human beings alone, but all living things." And he smiled suddenly, a frugal, neat-toothed and wrinkle-wreathed smile, because he saw that I was amazed.

"Everything?" I asked, awed in spite of myself.

". . . including plants," he said.

For a few moments, my mind reeled, processing the thought: stag-beetles; crocuses; Eskimos; pangolins; wandering albatrosses; Saint Bernards; mindless strands of seaweed; Bengalis; hammerhead sharks and ruby-throated hummingbirds; microbes and monsters.

". . . though we stop short of single celled organisms," he said, as if intercepting the drift of my truncated survey of life. "In fact, even now a case is being fought by an amoeba and will shortly be brought up in Parliament. Depending on that decision, we will change the rule perhaps."

"Why discriminate against amoebas?" I said still a little dazed at the revelation he had made.

"Of course," he said, "because it is not clear that they die. How to issue a death certificate for a life form which simply subdivides," he mused, almost to himself, sucking pensively on a scrap of food caught between his premolars. Obviously, this was the subject of feverish debate, the argument that raised factions and stoked the furnaces of human ire along the tube-lit corridors of the Bureau of Reincarnation. "It is not clear-cut with them," he said. "It will make a nuisance of the filing system. Already we are overworked. The stenotypists have threatened a protest march."

But by this time I had been recalled to the purpose of my visit and the issue at hand. "Meanwhile," I said, breaking into his argumentative reverie, "coming back to me. Consider how simple my case is, compared with that of a hydra or paramecium: here I sit, healthy and plump with life, entirely unlikely to subdivide or encystate. Isn't there any way to grant me my meagre request? Isn't it possible to slip someone a little consideration, grease a willing palm?"

The little man sighed gently and trained his eyes back on me. "Madam," he said, "that is what I have been trying to explain to you. This is only the office of files, of documented records; I could tell you which lives are eligible for enlightenment, which lives are vacant, which ripe for transfers, which doomed to a thousand rebirths. You could have the whole cosmos opened to you if you wished to know what was going to happen to which life. But the *actual* allocations, the *actual* decisions —" he shrugged poetically "that is not for us to worry about. That is done at the Transmigration Department."

I snorted at that. "The Transmigration Department! Don't speak to me of transmigration — I think that's just a convenient excuse you people have cooked up to avoid explaining what really goes on here." I was absolutely sure of my ground now because I had repeatedly been assured that my request could be dealt with at the Transmigration Department, but try as I might, I had been unable to find it.

"But yes, madam," said the Assistant Registrar, eyebrows atwitter with the agitation of having to prove his point, "it is on the seventh floor."

"Vicious libel," I said bitterly, "because there *is* no seventh floor. The stairs stop short at the fifth floor and when you try to climb any further you reach the terrace. I agree, there is some cause for confusion, because there is a mezzanine floor somewhere else and no one seems quite certain just how many floors the building has, but so far I have not had any reason to believe in the existence of a floor above the sixth."

"I am telling you, madam there is," said the man. A new expression had entered his eyes, a conspiratorial look, and of something overheard in the lavatory. "There *is* a seventh floor, but I will tell you a secret — it is not easy to go there. Permission restricted, secret passwords. In fact, we ourselves do not know how to go there. We only get the message and the directives. There is a rumour that some people have found a way to go there, but I cannot tell you myself, I do not know it." A note of embarrassment had crept in. "We have only a small part to play, madam. Keeping records, that is all. The rest we do not know."

A fly nattered by, I felt a tickle in my nose and the storm warnings of an imminent depression. It looked like the end of the road. There are some people who like to hammer on about what they want even when it is obvious that their's is a hopeless case. Sometimes they even manage to get their way, merely because the other person cannot bear to hear their arguments any longer. Well, I have never been that sort. I will persevere up to a point, but as soon as pursuing my goal requires me to lose my reasonableness I accept that I have been beaten and back down quietly. This point, I felt, had been reached in the Assistant Registrar's office and I resigned myself to the loss of a great expanse of time. I got up to leave and said, "I'll be going then."

In a gesture of courtesy which surprised me, the diminutive officer hopped out of his chair, escorted me to the door of his cubby-hole amidst the filing shelves and held it open for me. As I passed out through it, I heard a whisper, the merest breeze of speech: "Find the peon Gopal! He knows something." I turned in astonishment, but the door had closed irrevocably and though I knocked and hammered for ten minutes on it there was no response from within.

I will not document the course of my search for the peon. It seemed I wandered about that miserable building for hours, days or weeks, it was hard to tell. There was little or no variation whatsoever in the routines of the place from one day to the next. The lights remained on continuously and the staff worked non-stop shifts. The innards of the building were labyrinthine and it was rare to catch even so much as a glimpse of the outside world. I gave up searching for the peon at one point, only to find that it was equally impossible to relocate the entrance through which I had discovered this nightmarish place. It was therefore with considerable surprise and relief that, turning a corner at random, I discovered a lonely passageway, innocent of tube lights, with a row of windows down one wall.

The peon sat perched on a window-ledge, etched against the beams of dusty sunlight forcing their way in from between the loose slats of the shutters. He was sitting there, doing nothing at all and looked up languidly as I approached him. I recognised him at once from the descriptions and I lost no time in confronting him with my needs.

"You are Gopal the peon," I said to him. "You know something about the Transmigration Department and how to reach it. I have been looking desperately for that same department but cannot seem to find it." I had thought enough about what I would say to the peon and said it, now, almost easily. "If you can tell me this that I need to know, I will give you whatever of value I have with me now — my four gold bangles, my diamond earrings, my gold ring with the sovereign and, if they are not enough, I can — I can offer myself." Truly, I was desperate.

He looked up with that cynical all-seeing, all-knowing expression of peons who work in the halls of the mighty. With one glance he assayed the worth of my possessions, briefly considered the attractions of my person, weighed the true nature of my quest against his scale of values and made a spot decision. "I'll show you for nothing," he said, and got up to lead the way.

The route was, predictably, circuitous. We went down the deserted corridor, descended a flight of wooden stairs, crossed a fetid latrine crawling with unspeakable life forms, over a small wrought-iron bridge connecting two sections of the building — I had long since ceased to understand what manner of architect had been responsible for this monstrosity, it seemed to have expanded out of control. We passed by kitchens and warehouses, file clerks and laundry women, rooms full of Japanese tourists and bandicoots, rooms filled with windows, rooms empty with pigeons. . .

And along the way Gopal spoke to me about my quest. "You want to change your life," said the peon, as easily as if it were a switch in toothpaste brands. "You want to overturn the progression of reincarnation. You want to jump your place in the queue." He shrugged, worldly-wise. "It can be done."

He spoke as one who has learnt to see creation from a slightly remote and favoured position. "As for bribes, there are many ways to make them: sometimes a little incense, sometimes a few flowers, sometimes a handful of gold coins, sometimes a river of blood. They are easily bribed, on the seventh floor," he said, a little contemptuously. "Still," he continued, "they are only a different kind of clerk to the ordinary human ones. They can adjust a life here, a life there, but they cannot change the rules."

"But who can change the rules?" I asked, bewildered. I had thought that the seventh floor held all the answers, but annoyingly and like any other outsize concern, one could never seem to get to the real epicentre of things, no final resolution to one's curiosity. "What are the rules?"

The slight sense of unease that had first set in at the Assistant Registrar's cubby-hole had, by this time, settled into a compact mass of unhappiness. I knew, as I sprinted to keep up with the peon, that I was swiftly losing my grip on the situation. Running a specialised sort of travel agency for souls or changing your own life is all very well as long as it is under your own control but I was beginning to suspect that I would never really be shown or instructed in the actual process of the transfer. I had imagined some sort of machine, something like a large, friendly computer, with the Bureau's staff acting as its maintenance team. But with every passing second, the chances of ever reaching the machine or ever understanding how to operate it, were growing dimmer. I began to regret having got involved in this thing.

Also, I hated all the information that Gopal was giving me about the seventh floor. Whenever I asked him where the rules were set down and who could change them he would merely smile his dazzling smile and sweep on with his discourse, in the manner of someone who rarely gets a chance to hold forth on his favourite fixation. "Everyone knows they are terribly careless," he said. "One extra digit on the forwarding letter to the Registry of Rebirth and a pious zebra is reborn as a lusty dandelion, saints reborn as coral polyps in the Great Barrier Reef. They play terrible jokes: an incestuous couple reborn as kissing gourami, lovers reborn as Siamese twins, oysters reborn as misers."

"But," I said weakly and plaintively, as we negotiated yet another dark and slimy passage, "why are you telling me all this? I don't want to know. I don't want to hear about how corrupt they are in heaven and how meaningless it is to struggle on earth and how futile it is to live a decent life. I already know all that. It's within this futile life that I would, at the very least, like to live a rich and comfortable one — by whatever flea-bitten standards we have for such things back in the place where I live. I'm not interested in the larger issues — I just want this life, this one which I know about at this moment, to be vastly improved."

"Yes, yes," he said impatiently, running fleetly up a down-moving escalator, "that's where I am taking you, to the place where you will get a chance to improve your life." And he told me about angels and demons, ghouls and sprites, mountains of human ash, mansions of perfumed ice, pickled crab genitals and the thousand petalled lotus.

Another green door, a gust of wind and suddenly we are there at the seventh floor.

I gasped and said, "It's not at all as I expected it to be." But Gopal bustled me through, talking crisply all the time. "What I am going to do is this," he said, finally approaching the specific area of my interest. "I am taking you to the -- I call it the departure lounge. This is something I discovered for myself. I found the place where it actually happens, the exchange of life essence, from soul to flesh, and flesh back to soul."

I was amazed. "Aren't there any formalities to complete?" I asked, refusing to accept the truth about my situation, at the mercy of the peon. I wanted something reassuring to sign, something to guarantee me my own life back if I weren't satisfied, something to ensure that I wasn't being taken for a fatal ride by a power-hungry underling in an empire whose horizons now seemed to stretch from dawn to dusk. "How do I know you are not fooling me? How do I know you are not dying of cancer and are only awaiting your opportunity to grab my nice healthy body? How do I know you will not loan it out to your friends -- perhaps dead friends -- for free rides?" My mind had begun to fill with the various obscene and exotic horrors that this bureaucracy beyond all others seemed to offer. "How do I know you are who you say you are?"

But it was long past the time for second thoughts. The peon merely smiled lightly and ushered me into a corridor whose walls seemed to curve and melt and cease to hold their substance stable. Immediately and subtly, the atmosphere of an airport was created by a sense of current and urgency around us, by the blandness of the corridor and impression of hosts of fellow travellers crowding alongside us in patient yet determined strides. I could see no one except Gopal and myself but all around me I could feel the pressure, though not physical, of others. I was frightened then. I could smell them, these fellow travellers: seaweed and nasturtiums, warm cubs, hot butter, the pages of a new book. It was as if each one of them carried its own personal identity in the form of a distinctive scent. I felt arctic waters close about my stomach and my flesh begin to shimmer in an atmosphere dense with metaphysical beings. How do I smell, I wondered within me, what is my scent! Will I ever know it?

"What you have to do is very simple," Gopal was saying, matter of fact as ever. "I will show you where to go. You go there and then you wait, just as you might wait for the next airbus to Cochin. You won't have long to go."

"Just a moment," I said, terror flooding my inner ear. "I had very specific desires about the ways in which I wanted my life changed. What you suggest — I'm not even very sure what you suggest — sounds extremely haphazard. You've not explained anything about how the exchange is to take place, or what choices I am to get or by what means I am to make my selection. You haven't given me forms to fill or tickets to hold on to, or life jackets or airsick pills." The terror had reached my tonsils and was spilling out in little sparks and flashes, leaving a taste like ozone in my mouth. It seemed that the atmosphere around us grew increasingly thick with the passage of souls and I fancied I could feel them eddying irritatedly about me, confused at my physical presence yet fundamentally disinterested, hurrying onward to their embarkation gates. Every so often I would feel one push straight through me, leaving behind it an aftersmell of itself and my fear would increase a hundredfold. I felt the weight of each blood cell as it fled in panic through my arteries and I felt the labour of each separate bronchiole as it processed the heavy air I breathed.

My mind began to fill, slowly, with the red and throbbing manifestation of my own life. Dimly, as if at a distance, I could feel Gopal the peon take my hand and pat it comfortingly and say, "It's so simple: you wait a short space of time and then a moment will come when you will know you have to make your choice. At that moment all you have to do is to wish. Just wish. As you used to on falling stars and rabbits' paws." I clung dumbly to his hand, so friendly and solid in this concourse of odours and spirits and he repeated his advice. I looked at him, or tried to — I could not focus clearly. He had receded from sight, to become a dark figure, vaguely beside me. All around us, the silent traffic of spirits, souls in transit; throbbing in my head, throbbing in my hands and feet, in my blood.

We were almost there. I could see a haze ahead of me, as if the corridor (now barely perceivable in terms of walls and floors) were widening out, then suddenly we were in a vast hall, perhaps? a vast space, blinding white. I shut my eyes and abandoned myself to my terror, now flowing out freely in glowing lines from my ears, nose, eyes and navel. I could feel my blood, red and hot with life, pounding through the lacework of my veins and arteries, I could feel it in my neck and earlobes, across my belly and in the calves of my legs. I could feel, like distinct and terrible drum-beats, the double-clapping thunder of my heart's valves as they powered the life substance across the span of the small, warm and fragile world of my body.

It seemed as if that whole vast hall were filled with this thunder, the thunder of blood and life, the air vibrated with it. The boundaries of my body seemed to have already dissolved into the space around me so that the whole hall and all its spectral beings pulsed in rhythm to my drum-beat. I cannot say that I was truly conscious, but I could still feel Gopal pushing me firmly onwards, disengaging my hand and saying, "Don't worry, I will stay by your side. I will stay by you."

But of course he did not or I think he did not, because after a point my mind vaulted too far out of its normal orbit to know or care much longer. I heard him say. "You need only wait a short while and then you will step out of your own accord and when the moment comes, you will wish."

I had become a live and sparking bundle of fear, so clear and pure that it defined my entire existence. I did what I had to do, without question. Stepping out, I experienced what may have been a short wait or a long one. Then, as Gopal had explained, a moment came and silence fell about me like thunderbolts. I looked around me and meteors scarred and seared my eyes, stars shot away on either side of me like hailstones and my mind reeled with radiance. I felt the emptiness of the void collapse me, melt me down, I felt the mouths of a billion billion billion souls suck me in, assimilate me within their experience, renew themselves upon my life — then breathe me out with a whistling, steaming roar from their billion billion billion gorges. At that instant I knew I had to make my wish. I wished.

A SECOND'S BLINKING.

I looked up and saw the hot and shining sky. I looked down and saw — nothing. Nothing.

I was not there.

Perhaps, if I had had a body then I could have recorded the emotions that I felt at that moment in physical terms: the betrayal, the shock, the foolishness, the self-reproach. But instead, just like the lack of body, there was a lack of any feeling in the place where I would normally have registered emotions.

Already the Bureau, the people in it, the peon and the star-studded place were vanishing like a lazy dream and I would surely have dismissed it as one if it were not for my conspicuous loss of body. I knew then that I had been cheated and made a spectre of; but I did not feel in the least concerned as I hung suspended in the heavy air of mid-afternoon, people bustling about and through me. I drifted gently around, not caring where I went, sometimes passing through people, sometimes through buildings, sometimes through trees and dogs. I felt like a polite visitor at the art exhibition of a friend, neither moved by nor critical of the array of minds and lives presented to me.

Towards evening I found myself approaching the place where I used to live. I remained dispassionate and allowed the current to take me there of its own accord. I entered through the walls and settled into my own room.

As I sat there, lulled into a calm and peaceful mood by all the familiar artefacts of my distant life, I gradually became aware of a sensation at my feet — I suddenly became aware of my feet, the tingle of flesh and bone against the floor. I looked down to the place where I had been used to find them and felt an odd pleasure as I recognised them thickening slowly into substance. My feet, my hands, my head and navel, all of these and all that lay between them were, very gently and unhurriedly, rematerialising from the void. And in a short space of time I could sense all of myself, from the humblest capillary and hair root, to the muscles powering my heart, the small compact planet of my existence once more bonded together and ticking with its own familiar rhythms. I sat there in the gathering twilight of my room, with the warm thudding comfort of my life marking time within me, without me; and I felt, at that moment, a deep and savage bliss.

No Letter from Mother

VISHWAPRIYA L. IYENGAR

JUNE: THE MONSOONS had caught the trees by the throat and were shaking leaves down into basins of slush. I climbed the wooden staircase, pitter, patter, softly, with the crepe soles of new school shoes. Friday, Bangalore...

New Delhi would be hot, the dining table laid out with bunches of lichis, cherries and plums. My sisters would be laughing. Appa would return from court with chilled bottles of beer, and gladioli. The red flowers looked beautiful against his black coat.

"Holy Mary Mother of Christ, blessed is the fruit of thy womb..." I was late. "Always late," Sister Francis screamed, "in her last janam she must have been a tortoise." The letters had come, the red bag with the applique battleship was full to the brim, there would be a war over postage stamps.

The bag would spill out letters from France, Japan, Portugal, Morocco, Algeria, Sudan, Malawi, Tanzania, Ethiopia, Kenya, Kuwait, Dubai, Bahrain, Egypt, Singapore, Philippines, Thailand, Ireland and New

Zealand. From Kashmir, the coffee estates of Coorg, Nagercoil, Bombay, Calcutta, but these created no conflict, the stamps were common.

Sister Francis would reel the names off like a hymn and hand the letters out as if they were almond-honey pastries. Even best friends would part, rushing to secret cracks of sunlight, shade, and to suck the warm milk of concern. It taught us to loop words across continents, the crackling long-distance electricity spattered on paper.

The girl from Saigon never got any letters, she stood with her back to us, hands clenched like dead sparrows, her father was Vietnamese, her mother Tamil. Fabula never spoke to anyone, never laughed and never had any foreign goodies like chewing gum, chocolates or fancy pencils and rubbers.

Vietnam remained mute in our imagination. Her dresses had French chiffon pleated ruffles, but they looked shabby with washing, the dhobi had burned the fabric a bit, so it wasn't "foreign-foreign".

Shama, her father was a Collector in Nagercoil, told Fabula during dinner, "You are telling lies, you are not from foreign, Vietnam does not exist, you are Indian. Show me one stamp from Vietnam." Fabula stood up and screamed hysterically, "There is a War!" Shama laughed, "There is war in so many places but everyone still gets letters. . ." Fabula threw her custard on Shama's face and started to cry in a strange gasping way, "There is napalm, napalm everywhere. . ."

The new French nun came and took Fabula away, muttering something in French, Fabula responded in torn syllables of the same language, so we concluded

INTER·CONTINENTAL

HOTELS AND RESORTS

981-2740

Embassy
721-2951-9
721-2959

For reservations call:
London (0181) 847 2277 Outside 0345 581 444
These calls are charged at local rates

that she was really foreign after all. Shama is now our representative in the U.N. in New York, IFS and all that, she had led the discussion on napalm in the grotto.

Bougainvillaeas shook raindrops off crimson petals on our soft brown cheeks, rajnigandha grew at the Madonna's feet. We ate English toffees from Kenya. Shama said, "Napalm is a kind of Vicks, like the Malaysian Tiger Balm, maybe Fabula is a kind of orphan, that's why the French nuns are always running after her."

Fabula was taut, numb, back to the applique bag, her hair on edge. Fabula was afraid of getting a letter.

Appa would write me long letters, full of anecdotes from Birbal, Tenali Raman and Kautilya. Nothing could puncture his enthusiasm for anecdotal algebra. If I got bad marks, there would be a story, a rhyme, a proverb. If I did something horrid for which I was disgraced, Gladstone or Disraeli would come to my rescue. Nice envelopes, with markings of the Supreme Court Bar Association. "Be humble, be determined, be considerate." His adjectives flew flags, his letters were funny, but always that Gandhi stamp. My letters caused no commotion in the power-axis of stamp collectors. I read them on top of the haunted tree, in a hammock of long gnarled damp-brown branches, in the filigree greenlight from shimmering leaves. In the company of great men I learnt to say, "To hell with..."

I had not done anything recently which provoked compassionate comment, so Appa hadn't been able to dip into his magic bag of quotable quotes, he was beginning to sound a little boring, like Nehru. I was embarrassed to tell him, but I had read those letters to Indira in the library. There was no wit, no masala in the words, they were like boiled vegetables when you were sick. I wanted hot pungent words like the spices in the kitchen, roasted brinjal fragrant with cloves.

Mother never wrote me letters. Mother was always reading Kannada novels by women late at night; when she thought everybody was asleep she would read aloud. It was raining, I remember that passage:

Thick night, wet footprints of sorrow search a whole world for the meaning of the circle, flowers with scents of passion grow in your footprints, a snake comes and guards your vats of perfume, each moment of your absence, each mile of your distance sprouts succulent red petals in the earth. Search my beloved, for meanings. . . search till the edge of madness and despair, for everywhere the flowers grow in your footprints. Your body grows limbs of perfume in my memory. Like an eyelid, this door is open, return with threshed sheaves of meanings, my beloved, return with the golden wheat of love, return with ballads that turn your throat into bells. The world is an iron circle, does the lotus grow in the swamp of madness or in clear springs? This eye is open and waits to mate infinite meanings within your eyes. This is the threshold of the world.

This passage was one of many which Mother opened like steel doors at midnight when the house had been quilted to sleep in a soft blend of mixed breathing. Her voice was rich, it leapt through the air like Beethoven, they were pressed in my memory like exotic blossoms.

I learned to crumple self-esteem in moments of despair, to unfurl these passages with intensity and exhort them to release perfume in captivity. I longed to slide into the cave of warmth of her plump body, and calm my simmering loneliness in the music of her midnight words, but she never wrote.

"Holy Mary Mother of God, blessed is the fruit of thy womb..." Zarina from Zambia was passing a stick of Wrigley's Spearmint to Bina from Calcutta. I hope Appa was not hurt, I had written neatly on ruled paper last Sunday.

> Please Appa, I beg of you, ask Amma to write me a letter... anything, tell her she can shout also. Tell her to scold me because last week I did not do arithmetic homework, I talk too much during class, my keds were not blancoed properly, I am lazy to do work properly, I am always coming late for everything. During geography I am always dreaming of climbing into ships and wandering away into places on postage stamps, I want to go to Vietnam and rub napalm on my chest because I have a cold. I am not wearing my woollen banian during the rains, tell Amma, she will be angry.

Amma shouted with gusto, she turned metaphors with an iron ladle in a simmering black bowl of puliogray goj*. I bumped into her in the kitchen, she

---

* Tamarind sauce, seasoned with sesame and spices, to be mixed with cooked rice; a traditional South Indian dish which keeps for a long time.

barked, "Are potatoes sprouting from your eyes?" She heard me telling my sister something bad about a girl, and yelled, "Throw a stone into a shit-pit, it splashes on your face!" I hoped she would have got very angry, I hoped she would scold me lots and lots, spicy, in a fruit-bowl of ripe words.

Mother had never written me a letter during the three years I was in boarding school. The rosary was at its vernal equinox in Sister Francis' white liver-spotted hand, "Holy Mary. . ." Bina and Zarina were bubble-kissing ". . . fruit of thy womb. . ."

I hope Appa did not think I had become idiotic, I did like to have a meaningful dialogue with him, only those Nehru letters, they were like starched serviettes, not at all like Amma's soft voile pallav which kissed lips as you wiped them, there were stories in every pore of her body, in her last janam she must have been Valmiki. "Like an eyelid this door is open. . . this is the threshold of the world."

I wanted something dark, something shining, something wet, language like mother after her bath. I was lonely, I was talking to myself these days, images were marching towards poetry, every night I cried, I wanted someone to hold, someone's breathing to twine with mine, I was afraid of dormitories peopled with the dreams of so many children. I was running away from becoming like so many, I was running away from the herd.

"In the name of the Father, the Son and the Holy Ghost. . . Amen." The red applique bag was round and swollen like a pregnant woman's stomach, the letters came spilling out, Zambia, Ethiopia, Portugal,

Malaysia, Singapore. . . new alliances were made on the strength of postage stamps, friends fought and bubble-gum kisses turned to bubble fights. I was ready to push my dhow out into the picture of the world, like eyelids my doors were open. The letter did not have the Supreme Court Bar Association markings, a hesitant childish writing had fumbled over my name. The envelope smelt of cloves, roasted brinjals and midnight soliloquies in the quilt of breathing.

Mother had written me a letter! In my excitement I did not register Fabula trembling when her name was called, her about-turn in a military parade towards an execution fire. In my excitement I had not looked at the Vietnamese stamp.

The letter stayed warm and breathing in my pocket. It was still raining, I could not go to the haunted tree and anyway that was for Appa's letters, I had to find a special place to read this. That night I burrowed under my blanket and switched on my flashlight and opened the clove-fragrant envelope.

Amma had written,

My dear Ippiya,

> Many thanks for your letter dated. . . Please do not beg for anything, not even a letter from me. Appa writes good English letters. Please accept that. I cannot write in English. Your teachers will make fun of my English so I will not write again to you. We are sending you plums, please share with friends. Don't be bad girl, don't be lazy, don't dream in geography period. Don't ask me to write again.
>
> With love,
Amma.

I cried that night like I did every other night, a little more perhaps. I was too young to realise that colonisation had cut the bond twixt mother and child. The threshold of the world became a spasm of pain in my guts. I never forgave Mother but, in time, I learnt to open my own midnight doors, searching for footprints of a forfeited language. . .

I rubbed my tears with the letter, chewing the wet ball of pulp, I made it rounder and rounder. I wrote Appa a sensible letter the next day.

Fabula from Saigon never woke up in the morning, we heard the nuns whisper something about rat poison, no one knew what her letter had said. But now we knew that Vietnam existed, everyone had seen the stamp — except me.

Twilight

MANJU KAK

WHY THIS GLIMMER? This misty shape? Whose voice do I hear? Why is she calling me out of my sweet reverie? My glasses! Where are they? Ah, the shape becomes clearer now. Oh. . . it's bahu again. For a while I was with Sheila and we were playing kookie. We were in the aangan of our old Multan house and Amma was calling us in for tea. Juicy hot jalebis from the bazaar, she tempted. But they've backed away. Vanished. Just as she called. There are no jalebis here. Not ever. Just this worn wooden table, a glass of water and bottles of medicine.

My vision's blurred again. No, not tears, just water in my eye. What would an old woman like me do crying? What's left to cry for? There, that's better. I see her long hand clearly now. Long, hard, bony. Drink it, she commands quietly, pointing those harsh fingers at me like the whip of an ebony cane, her voice menacing beneath its camouflaged gentleness. As if I don't know what's around me. As if I was an invalid. Horlicks, they give me. Horlicks! Good for your health, they say.

Look at that cup. It's chipped. They don't trust me with their good china. They think I'll drop it. I pretend I don't notice these things anymore. I, Shanta, who took such pride in my housekeeping, who never wore a saree unless it was crisp with starch... and now I wrap them around, limp like yesterday's rotis! I used to give my clothes away the moment they looked a little weary. But now... the older, the softer she says, with that relentless look in her eye. Those spider black eyes of hers. What's the point, she tells him. Stains, full of stains, she spills everything.

Well, well, it's time to get up. These days I have to tell myself the morning's begun. Sometimes they just roll into one, night and day. At five sharp he used to go for his walk. A flower for me every morning. When will you stop this foolishness, I would tease him. Not till I die, he would say with his crooked smile. But he did. He went, and the flowers went with him too. C'mon old woman, rise. Why think of all that now. Rise, rise, lift leg, why don't you lift, a little higher, just a little higher. Aah, that's better. Into the slipper, first the big toe then the little ones; now raise yourself gently, Shanta. Rise. Stand firm. No, you will not falter. Not in front of her looking on.

A woman. I need a woman to look after me, I said. She refused. Small flat, she wants privacy, she says. What privacy! She goes nowhere, does nothing, just listens to foolish songs on the radio and hums in that tuneless voice of hers. Sex! That's all they ever do for fun. Whooosh, Shanta. If Amma had heard you! Amma... she too has gone. They have all gone. Oh, why didn't they take me, too.

They said, we'll manage Ma, when they sold my house. I told him it wasn't going to be easy. I was used to my ways. That's why I said, keep a woman for me. But he looked at her and chickened out. The expense, I heard her telling him. As always.

Whatever I need is expensive. Well, let them manage now. Now why look stern when I spill my tea? I'll spill it as much as I like. Let her wipe it. By god's grace my husband left me enough, but all they do is invest, Invest, INVEST all the time. They talk of shares and securities and deposits. And then he drools. And then they save. They don't live, these people. . . they. . . they simply calculate.

When will he take her away? Is there a God up there listening? Is this living? She lies in bed wetting six sheets a day, soiling her mattress. I have to get the office peon to help me take it up to the roof to dry. Now and then he will sullenly look me in the eye. Oh, but she doesn't think of all that. She's much too busy being unhappy. Lamenting her fallen state. Thinking of her old bungalow and the style she used to live in. I can feel her accusing eyes boring holes into my back even as she sweetly syrups, beta please do this, beta please do that. I know what she thinks and feels. Oh, yes, I know she hates me. So what difference does it make? I still have to look after her, don't I?

"If it's not too much trouble, a glass of water, beta." Look at how she resents doing my chores. It's not as if I'm asking much. Not a smile on her face. It's as if it was made for mourning. Neem. That's what she looks like. As bitter as the neem datun. There she comes bringing it. God knows if she's put poison. I'd better sip and see. No, it tastes alright. One can never be too sure though. They might get it into their heads to get rid of me. Aah, but I'm a match for them still. It won't be so easy. What if they put it into my tea? Yes, tea possibly. But tea the cook brings me. I know he's on my side. I see it in his eyes. He's more gentle than that fat man who lolls on the sofa. Son! All he talks to me about is money. Oh yes, he comes in when he wants me to sign something. A jailor, that's what he is. . . oops, the spittle.

— Hanky! Where's my hanky! Vicky, Vicky, Vicky, VICKY! He can hear me alright. I know it. He's hiding somewhere. VICKY!

— Yes, Dadi! *There she goes again. Right in the middle of my game.* Coming, Dadi.

— Now he answers. I know he heard me straight off. And they think I've grown senile. Hanky, beta, where is it? One of you keeps fiddling with my things. How many times I've. . .

— Right next to you, Dadi.

— Ah. . . yes, I have it now. . .

Hai ram, I sit here all day bored to tears. But what else is there to do! Read, she says. Read what? Read the trash she gets me? The same books over and over again. Get me the old authors.

The library has no more, she says. Buy them then, I tell her. I used to. Belonged to the Book Club. I had them all, the best-sellers, but they wouldn't let me bring them! No space in the flat she told him. There's space enough for her stupid music, isn't there!

The sun's growing warm. I think I'll go in for a bit. Tired Shanta. Easily tired, huh?

Aah... the bed... my refuge. Oh dear, I need to go to the bathroom. Why didn't I remember a minute ago, before I lay down. Now to get up again, to lift myself... to reach out. No, no... no no, NO... fhoof... I tr... the release... ah, the heavenly release... and... the trickling warmth... it spreads... up... up my petticoat. Oh now, now it begins to feel cold. I must get up and change. I must rise and change... I must... oh leave it, just turn over, it'll dry up soon... the angels beckon, Shanta, the angels come... is that you again... sister Sheila?

Again she's wet her bed. Pretending she did it in her sleep. Just laziness, sheer laziness. Time and time again I've told her to use the toilet before lying down, but will she ever listen? Just plain cussedness. When will it end! Sometimes I think I'm at the end of my tether. That instead of her it'll be I losing my mind. You make too much of it. She's an old woman. How can I explain it to him... the way I feel. It's not as if he's home the whole day to see what happens. It goes on and on and on... day after day after day... just entering her room... the smell... oh, the smell... and if the door is left open she screams out she's cold.

— Vicky, Vicky...
— *There she goes again.*
— Vicky!
— Go, beta.
— Ma, I'm in the middle of...
— Vicky, Vicky...
— Go, beta.
— You go...
— She wants you. Go, GO, beta.
— Don't shout, I'm going.

— Now what, Dadi.
— Slow the fan, Vicky. No, now it's too slow, faster one, just one, no, that's too fast. Now it's right.
All the time she wants something. Can I go now?
— Yes, dear.
— What did she want?
— The fan.
— Did she say anything?
— No, why?
— Just asked.
That's the way it is all the time. Something or the other. I think I must get out. But what's the use, I'll have to come back. And then it feels worse. Damn. I'm young, why should I feel this way. But she stretches her hands my way, pulling me into her world of aches and pains and feebleness and worse, the resentment colouring all I think and do. I mustn't allow myself to be dragged in. Look at her skin. Smooth and creamy still. A good life she's had. And mine? Sallow. Fine lines drawing an artist's rough sketch on my forehead. Today it's no gas, tomorrow the buses are late, day after it's the milk vendors' strike. Distances, moody servants. The way I have to wheedle and cajole to keep the help. Times have changed, I tell her. But how would she know and what does she care? Her meals on time. . . her bath water hot. . . her bed made. . . that's all she thinks about.

Vicky. . . bahu. . . bahu, Vicky. . . they're not listening again. . . I know they're there hearing me call, listening to me breathe, listening to me as I slowly fade, measure by measure, but do they care? There's life in me still. I'll show them yet. I shall make them wait before they can hoist me away and lay hands on what is mine. Oh yes, I shall show them. Bahu, Vicky!

... where is everyone... hide and seek they'll play... well, I'll tackle them my way. I'll not bide them any longer... I'll not take my pills. I'll not go to the toilet... I'll not... hush... hush, Shanta, hush... there it is... I can see it clearly... my old home... the verandah... and my chair... who put it out... why, foolish girl, it's mali of course... mali. Mali..! Oh, there he is watering the last of the winter blooms. I must remind him to collect the seeds before they wither away and store them in the shed with the lily bulbs... the dahlias did well and so did the candy tuft, but the pansies... Pannchoo warned me, try the other nursery, he said... next year... yes... maybe next year... now where has he disappeared... watering the crotons, is he? Soon the summer winds will blow and he will have to bring them into the shade; yes, the winds will blow hot and dry and the green grass wither into hues of dull brown... and my beautiful flowers will... but... no... there'll be life still... the mango blossoms will sprout little green fruit and the mali's son will shoo away the parrots that come to peck at them. Ah, yes, though the lawn may wither ... there'll be other things to see. And I can still sit the evenings out... in my chair... looking on... watching the seasons change in my garden.

Dooz, Charu and the Establishment

SUBHADRA SEN GUPTA

I MET HIM again on a grotty Janpath sidewalk while going past a man selling chaat, stepping gingerly across discarded paper plates. A disgusted, disembodied voice said from somewhere below, "Where's your moustache, Dooz?" I looked down at him. "What have you done with it?" he asked in anguish.

"I donated it to the FAO," I said, the old repartee coming back beautifully, "it'll fertilize jute fields in Bangladesh."

He applauded my sally, then patted the kerbstone beside him and said companionably, "Squat, love."

I glanced down at my genteel polyester saree, my strappy chappals, the elegantly swinging wool coat. "I'm respectable today, dummy. And I'm carrying these madly important office files."

"Give them to him," pointing to the chaatwala. "He's run out of madly important paper plates." Then more vehemently, "C'mon, Dooz. Sit willya, please."

It's pointless arguing with him anyway. So I perched beside him. From the kerb one gets rather an interesting angle of vision of shoes and legs and car wheels.

"When did you come back?"

Ignoring my question he turned to face me fully. A rough hand raised my chin, two curious eyes surveyed my skin. "You look like the Establishment," he said. And then sniffing my perfume, "You smell thought-provoking."

"Sorry. But what didja expect? You leave for Londontown and me left alone to carry on."

He checked my pulse. "And your pulse is socially relevant."

I felt terrible. Here was Charu holding my hand after seven years and my pulse had to be so treacherous. He let go of my hand, waved at a passing Mercedes, flapping a flag, with an ambassador inside, and said, "Dooz, they treat you good? You still alive or they killed ya?"

"Barely. I need you real bad."

"My junk?" looking pleased.

"Your peerless, utterly scintillating junk."

"Your vocabulary's improved. *Scintillating*. Next you'll say trip to the *exotic* land of the *mysterious* Orient."

"Buy the jet plane tickets at *attractive* rebates with *smiling* airhostesses." And we laughed like hyenas. Such pure oxygenated junk. It felt good to be back.

Dooz and Charu. Durga Sen and Girish Chari. We were a good team once. A healthy, junky, brainless, destructive team. We killed a lot of progressive, socially committed people in stealthy ambush.

Now it was my turn to pick holes. I pulled his face around by the ear. The rebellious moustache, whipping eyebrows, perpetual-motion eyes. On his face I caught no whiff of the dreaded Constructive Progress. It was still real, alive and normally out of control. The cheeks were thinner, a new scar on the temple, an earring in the left earlobe. "What's the verdict, hizzoner? I pass the physical? I join the Great Indian Army?" Then, flexing his arms, "My biceps are rocklike. My patriotism stern and. . ."

I stopped him from springing up. "No! You will not sing the National Anthem."

That's an old malady. Serenading passing cows or motorists in dark glasses to the anthem. The cows being bovine need education, the motorists are KGB and are to be uplifted to our path of non-violence. "I fail you, Char. Your shoes are the wrong colour, your papa's not a managing director and you don't know the capital of Nicaragua."

We had acquired an audience by now. Charu always does. It is something to do with the psychic emanations from his wirewool hair and also because he is so patently, simply, absolutely sane. Children always watch him carefully for signs of breakdown into adult behaviour.

A little girl of about nine, carrying a tray of hairclips and combs, and a boot-polish boy stood looking intently on. Charu called them closer. He bought me a pair of pink and purple hairclips and the boy polished his dusty boots. Then he gave them a tenner each from my purse, pulled me up, and we walked smartly into a crowd before the kids recovered.

"Always bunk from the business transaction." (The Complete Quotations of Charu.)

He sat down on a patch of grass in the centre lawn, lit a reefer, opened a file and read sheet after sheet of an exciting report on a scintillating sales promotion drive. Then he looked up, "This is suicide, Dooz. Euthanasia. EXIT with dignity. They killed ya."

That hurt, coming from Charu. He glanced at my face, picked up my hand and kissed my palm. "Forgive me, Dooz. They attack women harder. Those joint-stock company saviours of mankind. You need the howitzer, the anti-social missile. Much more than me."

"You still fighting the MPs, Charu?" MPs, those springing from the Mass of the Populace, Committed Beings, talking of the Motherland, Duty and smoking cigars. Sometimes, when he had the money, Charu smoked cigars too, for that jazzy MP look.

He did not answer. Instead he picked a dozen blades of grass and put them between the pages of the file. That's an old habit too. It was to fumigate the pages of the deadly pellagra — the world of Research & Development — that shrivels your brains and kills your eyes.

As I walked away Charu was lying on his back with a handkerchief over his face humming softly. I left the grassy file on my boss's Establishment desk to clear up the smell of social relevance.

When I reached the spot of Charu's last appearance it was growing dark and the grass was undisturbed. Under a tree a palmist was studying his fingertips. Charu would be rich one day, marry a tall, healthy, fair girl and live abroad. Charu crossed his palm with silver from my purse and laid a heavy arm on my frail dark shoulders. "Dooz, I can't help it, darling. Papa wants a fair girl with the rich horoscope." Then he kissed my neck and said, "Let's eat."

I checked the cash in my purse. Charu peered into the mess of handkerchiefs, bus tickets and bubblegum wrappers and fished out a pencil and a crumpled postcard. He settled on a stone seat and began to scribble, head bent industriously. We posted a letter to our old friend Keshav. They killed him at a medical college. Those vulgar prole medics didn't like his open eyes. So they hung him upside down from a window and stripped him naked. They killed his gentle body too, ten years ago. We are survivors, Charu and I.

I counted the cash. Thirty-two rupees. Charu was emptying his pockets. He pulled out a yellow visored cap and put it on and then rained loose change on a handkerchief. "Eight hundred and seventy paise." And he poured it all into my purse. He had stolen or borrowed a mobike from somewhere, a battered dragon with a monstrous roar. I froze behind him as we whipped through the streets.

At a dhaba under the Jama Masjid steps Charu sat wreathed in smoke over biryani. He lent me his reefers, they never taste as good without him.

"When did you come back?"

He blew a stream of smoke into my eyes. "I haven't come back yet, Doozy."

Straight on would get no answer, so I went at it angled and sly.

"You meet the Queen and the Prince in London-town, Char?"

He pulled his cap over his eyes and sniffed delicately at a plastic flower from the vase on the table, "The Queen adores yellow roses."

"And you meet the Oxford dons?" circuiting home.

His eyes were dreamy, "The spires of Oxford are dipped in the blood of brown Indians." And he threw the flower at a passing waiter with a poofy smile, "Shut up, Dooz. I killed Oxford."

All the unaccustomed reefers, food, Charu; things were getting a bit hazy for me. I remember Charu squatting beside a chowkidar warming himself by a little fire and sharing his chillum of ganja. The chowkidar approved of Charu's professional hold on the chillum. Then we were on a deserted lawn ahead of India Gate and it was past midnight. In the icy cold we saw a sardar icecream man going home.

"I think I'll go into dreaded commerce, Dooz, I'll sell icecream and I'll die before you. The MP's will get me."

"They've got me already. I get a salary and I'm polite."

"You say `Yes sir'?" he queried. I nodded. "And How is your wife's prostate, sir'?"

"Women don't have prostates," I said severely.

We had reached the Rajpath crossing and Charu climbed into the bowl of the dried broken fountain and pulled me up beside him. He scrambled atop a piece of broken sandstone, raised an arm and said, "Dooz, the pose right for a leper politician?"

I clapped. "Speech, Honourable Minister."

Charu cleared his throat and lit a reefer, "I have only one thing to say. Write it down, Dooz. Children of the world unite! You have nothing to lose but your Board Examinations."

He jumped down and came to sit beside me. We sat dangling our legs across the fountain rim watching lonely cars crawl by. Charu had gone quiet and withdrawn. I leaned against him, a familiar tiredness seeping through my body. The kind that hits you when all the junk gives out and you know the MPs wait for you at daylight.

"Will you stay awhile, Charu?"

He answered after a long pause. "No."

"Where will you go? The MPs are everywhere. You can't really escape."

"Who escaped?" he said. "They'd put me in a nuthouse if they could. I just don't let 'em."

"Who?" I asked astonished, all the wit and chit-chat deserting me. Charu wasn't junking, he was serious.

"The clan. The Daddyji and dear adored brother." I could feel him rigid against my leaning arm. I sat there trying to phrase a question he would answer. I couldn't risk his disappearing behind his junky hyperbole again. "Charu," I stopped to take my breath. "What do the MPs look like in Londontown? They carry briefcases?"

"Yah," he yawned. "And hold little note-pads and sit beside your bed."

"And they carry pills?"

"Pills and long needles and coloured capsules."

I looked down at my shaking hands and then peered carefully at Charu. His profile under the tilted visor was etched against the streetlights and I wished I could stop probing and make him smile again. "And when you came back to Delhi last autumn. . ."

He turned to look at me and his smile hurt. "Last week, Doozy. British Airways. The airhostess thought I was cute. Not loony at all."

"You're not loony," I said, trying to verbalize something for which even my fertile brain has never found any words. "Just different. Free and different."

"Then why did they give me those electric shocks?"

I had to say something. Any damn thing. Charu never understood silence. "That's an MP torture chamber, love. The conformist's home from home. You lost the battle, but" I said with emphasis, "we'll win the war. You just wait and see."

He snaked an arm around my waist. He is trying to comfort me, I thought in astonishment. "They lost the battle too, Doozy. I slimed out and flew away."

"Ambushed the buggers, didja Char?" I tried very hard to laugh normally.

"Right. And I'll ambush the clan, too."

How do you ask a person like Charu about the future, plans, careers, Oxford degrees?

"And those Oxford spires, Char?"

"Here's some bad news," he said, very effectively blocking my breath somewhere near my spleen. "I wore the mortarboard, Doozy. I walked the plank as the proles cheered and I got the white roll of paper."

"Oh, shit," I said, working hard at the disgust. "You get them bourgeois degrees and then you let the torture chamber get you. Where's your self-defence, Chari?"

He was silent again. Charu had told me all he would ever tell. There won't be any more information. I thought of Charu seven years ago. Whooping with delight when the letter came with the scholarship.

"Stay here, Charu. Please." I had run out of funny lines.

"Too many MPs around," he said. "But I'll come back to watch your progress."

"Progress?"

"Fight them for me, Doozy, until I come back with them special weapons."

"You will come one day?"

"One day."

Portrait of a Childhood

SHAMA FUTEHALLY

FROM THE BEGINNING we knew that our home was different. It was, of course, indefinably different from the homes of our school friends, as we saw whenever we went on visits. There seemed to be some uncomprehended gap between our home and the blue walls, stainless steel pans, and mothers barefoot in the kitchen, which is what we saw in the homes of our friends. There were other friends whose houses were somewhat like our own — where the table was laid with linen and there were potted plants and cut flowers and a clean servant bringing refreshments on a tray. Nonetheless it was true that our home and garden were uniquely beautiful, and this was clear even to a child. The front door opened on to a sitting room, mute but gay, in dark blues and browns with a low stone wall and french windows in front. These led on to a verandah which had low, cool benches made of large slabs of smooth stone; and beyond that was a garden so exquisite, so genuine, as to be hardly believable. In the evenings especially, as the long rays of the sun brought into focus its smooth surfaces of lawn, its dark and light patches, its thick clumps and light stone paths, its pond with the lilies and the kingfisher, my ten-year old heart used to suffer at the sight of it.

And beyond the garden were fields with toddy palms, with not another house in sight except that of our cousins where we would go to play. A mud road led around the fields, and there was also a mud path through them which was our "short-cut". Both roads seemed very much our own, there was hardly ever anyone else using them. In a way the fields seemed our own too, they went with the house and the garden, as the right kind of setting. But as we grew older we heard more and more frequently that there were "squatters" in the fields. The grown-ups used to joke about it, about sitting in the garden with their backs to the fields because of the "squatters"; and figures carrying rusty kerosene tins and disappearing behind the toddy palms became a common sight. When we had visitors we felt very ashamed. The little alcove in the sitting room where we had breakfast looked directly out on to the fields; sometimes the scene was bad and if we had a guest staying we had to apologise with charm. By the time I was twelve or so, I had learnt to do so myself in case my mother was not around.

Nevertheless, it had never occurred to us that the fields might disappear, that somebody else might want them and take them. When we first began to hear that "buildings" were going to be put up in the fields, a sort of dread made itself felt in the conservation, and nobody said very much about it. For my twelve-year old self and my ten-year old sister, it meant a first stirring of awareness that things which ought to be in our hands were not so, that fields which we wanted and liked, and which we ought to have, could be so completely outside our control. That other people were taking them over, that they were going to cut off our lovely view and put up buildings, was something I hardly allowed myself to imagine. But whenever I did think of "buildings", I had at the back of my mind large, clean buildings with marble fronts, like the ones in town. The truth was still to be learnt.

Meanwhile, our lives revolved very largely around our Ayah, to whom we clung, literally, all through our early years. She was large and fat and unchangeable, in her white sari. It was only slowly that I realised that she was a small bent woman, and not even particularly fat. She had a smooth fair face with a thick ugly nose which always bothered me; I felt that if only I could take it away and put another nose in its place she would be perfect. That Ayah was only human, and therefore subject to change, became apparent on the day she was mysteriously taken somewhere in a car and brought back wearing spectacles, which gave her a funny little squirrel face like an illustration in a children's book. "Now you won't get headaches any more," said my mother. But we looked at Ayah, giggling and ashamed and feeling that the world was not quite the place it used to be; and, to our dismay, Ayah looked rather sheepish herself.

In any case a sort of change had begun. One day I saw with surprise, while drinking my afternoon glass of milk, that my head came up to Ayah's shoulder and that I would soon be as tall as her; it was as if a little block in my mind had suddenly fallen into an empty slot with a bump. Because, as I had explained seriously to my cousin at the age of four, my parents were as tall as the toddy palms and Ayah was nearly as tall, but not quite. And now all at once I was nearly as high myself. Also, I was slowly beginning to see that there were curry stains on her saris, they were not really white, and the blouses were always torn under the armpits. And there was a peculiar smell whenever Ayah hugged us, and I began to wish that she wouldn't.

Now Ayah was the aunty of Paul, who cooked and chauffered. Paul was a hero to end all heroes. He could carry us on his shoulder all the way to our cousins' He could play gulli-danda as no one else could. He used to buy us sweets while driving us to school, and his jokes were the best in the world. "Bas!" we used to say, as he ladled food onto our plates. "No bus here," said Paul, "bus at the bus stop." And he would whisk away the dish on his palm, leaving us paralysed with admiration. He was usually in a vest and khaki shorts and had a little silver cross tied on a black thread round his neck. He had a shadowy string of brothers and sisters, nine or ten of them, and he would forget all their names as none of us would ever have dared to do. We were never tired of asking the name of his youngest sister, and hearing in reply, "Lora, or Phlora, some such."

"And where does she live?"

"Oh, somewhere good."

When the great Ayah Disaster took place, we minded more because of Paul than because of Ayah.

It happened like this. We had a visitor staying with us, an awesome intellectual English lady who nonetheless had beautiful leather bags, soft high-heeled shoes and a pink frilly thing to wear round her shoulders while she put on her make-up. I used to watch her mutely from a distance and wonder what it would be like to be her. One day I heard her saying to my mother, in the sort of English which belonged to another world, "I'm terribly sorry to have to say this, but I think one of your servants may be dishonest." Then there was a huddled conversation between them and I crept away. And about half an hour later we heard unusual screams and shouts in the backyard and ran there to see a dreadful sight. There was Ayah, hair dishevelled, standing small and alone on the gravel, throwing her arms about and shouting. Everyone else had gone away. Paul, in the kitchen, was looking miserable and pretending not to hear. "After fifteen years! Just because a foreign memsaab says something!" shouted Ayah. And we, who had always been on Ayah's side, we stood there dumb, on the wrong side of the battle. There was a moment when Ayah's red wet eyes met mine, and neither of us knew what to do. Ayah and I, who had always been the best of pals! My sister and I went away, leaving her shouting in the empty backyard. We never saw her again.

Meantime, the buildings were going up. I had assumed that one day we would just wake up and find large cool buildings around our house, with potted palms, a chowkidar, and shiny cars in front, but slowly the terrible truth began to dawn. It all began with a fat paan-chewing man wearing a blue nylon shirt and dark glasses, who arrived in a jeep one day, while two other people measured the ground with a tape and wrote things in a book. Rapidly, trenches were dug, they filled up with rain water in the monsoon, and an assortment of cement-coloured men, women and children arrived with their pots and pans and began to live under small pieces of coloured plastic or strung-up sacking. Green and pink saris were hung up to dry on the large water pipes in one corner of the field. I still thought that after it was all over the buildings would be beautiful, like those in the clean haven of "town", twenty miles away. But one day my father said casually, "Well, this is hardly worse than what it will be once it's finished," and at once I knew that the buildings, too, were not in our hands, that they would be like the other buildings in the neighbourhood, with three or four grimy floors each, large black patches caused by the monsoon, and with clothes hanging all over them. And I felt sick with despair. I was slowly learning that it was no use expecting other people to be like us, that they were inexcusably different, that one had to twist and turn one's way through them in search of others who were proper people like we were. And as for the wonderful world which existed in books — the Famous Five and their adventures, the "smashing" fun they had at their "super" school — of that I could only dream, whenever I managed to take myself off to the swing at the bottom of the garden, to get away from the world in which I had to live.

Portrait of a Childhood

And that happened more and more often, and for longer and longer periods. One day we were sitting in the garden in the evening, which we resolutely did in spite of the skeletal structures that were coming up all around us. Suddenly there was a barrage of little stones from the air -- we turned to look -- and there, laughing away, were half a dozen little labourers' boys sitting on the unfinished balcony of one of the buildings, with their fists obviously full of pebbles, all sniggering. Our anger and horror are hardly to be described. Somebody spluttered, "This is what happens when you lift them out of their proper station." I went off to the swing to forget not just that scene, but also what the future would bring.

Yes, that swing, on which I learnt to swing so rhythmically and so dangerously fast was becoming more and more necessary. Whenever anything happened which I wanted to drive out of my mind I rushed to the swing. There was, for instance, the day when I saw Mr. Ghote having his lunch.

Mr Ghote was my father's typist, which means that he sat in a small room in the factory premises which were not far from us. He was a tall, morose-looking man who was kind to me, giving me a sweet occasionally or letting me have sharpened pencils with rubbers attached. One day I went there at lunchtime with my father and saw Mr Ghote huddled among his papers with his tiffin carrier -- one of those with several small round boxes. As we came in he looked embarrassed and tried to hide the carrier behind his desk. It seemed to contain a brownish vegetable and two thick chappatis; and it was so clear that he was ashamed of them that I wanted to run away. At such times the swing was my only refuge. . . I would run to it, begin to swing, and hurriedly remind myself that Mr Ghote probably had quite a lot of happiness in his life after all. Indeed I was becoming quite adept at doing this — anything I wanted out of my mind — and it was done like the pressing of a button. Increasingly, there were sights or episodes which caused a helpless mixture of feelings. If I saw a young woman from among the labourers holding a howling baby, and crying to herself, I would hardly know what I was feeling, but whatever it was I wanted it out of my mind at once. If I couldn't get it out I would feel angry. This anger, to tell the truth, interfered a great deal with my peace of mind which, in any case, was hardly peace of mind any longer. Quite often I didn't know exactly what I was angry about. If someone were scolding a servant, I would be angry with them for being angry and angry with the servant for looking so miserable. And it took me hours to recover.

One year we were taken to Kashmir on a holiday. By this time, aged fourteen, I did not expect much enjoyment from life, it seemed to consist mostly of things which one had to avoid. But such enjoyment as was possible was surely all compounded in such an event as going to Kashmir. We were to fly there, another glamorous prospect. On the morning we were to leave I got up especially early so as to squeeze all possible enjoyment out of the day.

We left for the airport by seven. But my father had made a most unfortunate remark just as we were leaving. "What we are spending on this holiday would feed several families for a year," he said. I was trying to get this out of my mind as Paul chauffered us out of the lane, and there in front of us was a queue at the milk booth, and Mr Ghote standing in it. He had his empty bottles in a blue and white striped cotton bag. I told myself hurriedly that Mr Ghote could not be allowed to interfere with this occasion of all occasions and I resolutely prepared to enjoy myself to the full. But somehow the enjoyment had become very elusive. There we were, as dreamed of for several days, waiting in the airport lounge to go by plane to Kashmir. But in some way I felt dreary about it, the airport was too dusty and the plastic of the seats too red. On the flight, too, I waited unrewarded for some pleasure to emerge from the fact of the grey-blue seats, the complimentary sweet, the meal all wrapped up in plastic. And that evening I was looking out of our hotel window in Srinagar at the Dal Lake lit by fairy lights and feeling unmistakably dead, as I was to do for many years to come.

Thanks, anyway

ACHLA BANSAL

IT'S ETCHED IN my memory forever, my first visit to the crematorium. His cremation. Nothing much to cry about, considering he was a ripe 79. But when I thought of his bubbling laughter, his joie de vivre, his burning desire to meet his son and grandchildren, I was filled with, not pity — one could never pity him, even though he led a solitary life — but sorrow. How can one feel sorrow for a total stranger (that's what he was, till that brief encounter in a restaurant) my husband asked again and again. I could not explain to him why I no longer felt like celebrating my 29th birthday.

How cheerful I had been in the morning. I had baked two cakes, one for my family and one small one for our coffee session. It was a daily ritual. Five days a week, I drove up to his sprawling bungalow to share a cup of coffee with him. The maid kept it ready before departing and since he liked it piping hot, I dared not be late. I intended surprising him with the cake, for I had kept my birthday a secret from him.

Instead it was I who was in for a shock. He had been

found dead in his favourite rocking chair, by the maid. A small crowd had collected by the time I reached. Nobody knew what to do. In fact, they were all waiting for me to arrive.

I was in a quandary. Shouldn't I inform his son in the U.S., but. . . he had made me promise that in case he died, I would cremate him without waiting for his son to arrive. "I want to be cremated the same day and my son can never make it. And remember, no relatives," he had warned. "You're not dying just yet", I had tried to brush the matter aside. "I'm 78", he had persisted, "and at that age, one never knows. Not that one can be sure at any age. Death snatched away my younger son at the tender age of five. . ." The next moment he was laughing at the maid's three year old chasing a squirrel, while I sat brooding over his dead son. . . what if he had lived. . .?

The neighbours watched curiously as I went about making the necessary arrangements. Many eyebrows were raised, but I didn't care. He had never cared. Not when he ate alone in a jazzy joint frequented mostly by the younger generation, his feet tapping to the beat of "The way you make me feel."

He did not care if people sniggered at his natty clothes or wondered at his voracious appetite. I smiled as I recalled our first meeting, him dressed in spotless white, even the shoes were a sparkling white and the handkerchief. . . How it got deposited in my purse remains a mystery till this day. It was after a shopping spree that I had decided to treat myself to a much deserved lunch. Depositing my various packages on a chair, I opened my purse to take out my handkerchief, was wiping away my perspiration when a stern voice said accusingly, "That's my handkerchief you're using, young lady."

Astounded, I looked up. . . and then at the handkerchief. Good god, it was a gent's kerchief. "But. . ." I spluttered.

"And this happens to be my table. I left my handkerchief here. . . I, of course, didn't think of kleptomaniacs," he whispered. Blushing furiously, I began collecting my packages.

"You can share my table if you want to," he went on magnanimously, settling down with his soup.

"You don't mind sharing your table with a thief?" I said coldly.

"Tut-tut, I never called you a thief. A kleptomaniac is not a thief," he said smiling roguishly.

"Well, for your information, I am neither," I said haughtily.

"Can I have my handkerchief back?" he laughed.

To my horror, I realised I was still clutching it in my hand, and mortified, I handed it to him.

He chuckled. "Now how do I remove this lipstick mark? Not that it matters, now that my dear wife is no more, but. . ."

I snatched it from him. "I'll have it washed and sent to you," I declared loftily.

"I'll gift it to you. Why don't you keep it as a souvenir?" he guffawed.

"Certainly not. If you'll be kind enough to give me your address, it will be delivered to you," I said irritably. This whole business of a measly handkerchief was beginning to get on my nerves. Never had

I been so embarrassed in my life. Kleptomaniac indeed! What would my children say if. : . I shuddered. Despite his pleas to share his table I walked out on a hungry stomach, his address scribbled on my palm.

If it hadn't been for my determination, I would never have been able to locate his house. But I would have gone to any godforsaken place to return the darned handkerchief, so cut up was I about the whole episode. I cursed him all the way for leaving me to find the house on my own. He could at least have told me its whereabouts.

A sprawling dilapidated bungalow with a faded name plate was his abode. I looked around dubiously. There was nobody to be seen. After ringing the bell in vain, I was about to depart when I sighted him, sprawled on a rocking chair, dozing under the neem tree. As I stood about, wondering how to wake him up, he stirred, adjusted his spectacles and drawled, "So you've managed to hunt me out. Persevering, aren't you?"

"Here's your handkerchief," I said stiffly.

His eyes crinkled as he burst out laughing.

"Why are you so annoyed about the whole thing? It happens, you know. It's the funny side of life. If it weren't for these relieving moments, life would be such a bore, wouldn't it?" he smiled disarmingly at me.

Suddenly a weight lifted off my chest. It *was* funny. I began to laugh, and he joined in.

"Ah, you've managed to remove the lipstick," he smiled with satisfaction, inspecting his handkerchief.

"It happened a long time back... I was returning from office, when a young girl waved to me to stop. As a rule, I never gave lifts, but something about her made me stop. She looked so vulnerable. I started giving her a piece of my mind about thumbing lifts, when to my horror, she burst out crying. 'What are you sniffing about?' I scolded. 'At least use your handkerchief'. 'I have lost it,' she cried, rummaging in her bag. I gave her mine. After that all hell broke loose when my wife spotted the lipstick on my handkerchief. She kept asking where it came from. No amount of explaining would pacify her... poor soul," he sighed.

Time fled as we sat chatting. I promised to come again. And so began our 11 o'clock friendship, as we called it. Many a time, I prepared a snack and carried it over to have with our coffee. He showed me around his garden with maternal, or should I say, paternal, pride. What would happen to his plants if he should die, was his sole worry. Not that he thought about dying often. It was only when he was in a reflective mood that he talked about it.

"You know, it's been five years since I saw Nikhil — my son. In the beginning, he came every year, but now... he's too busy, I suppose. He's doing well, has property there... Why would he care for this ramshackle old house?" he mumbled, more to himself than to me. But I heard. "He could at least care about his father," I retorted.

"Oh, he does. He's forever sending me gifts."

"But he can't come and see you?"

He kept silent and an expression of pain flitted across his face. Suddenly he looked old, more than his

78 years. I never broached the topic again. He, too, avoided talking about Nikhil, till his letter arrived. Then he could no longer contain himself. He talked and talked, of his Nikky, his childhood, his grandchildren. "Don't they look like Nikky?" he said excitedly, showing me their photographs. I smiled at him wanly. I didn't have the heart to tell him that they had gone after their mother.

Sometimes instead of our scheduled one hour, we sat talking longer and on reaching home I worked in a frenzy, trying to make up for the lost time. My husband who came home for lunch, then had to make do with a meal of sorts. He naturally felt annoyed. "What the hell can you talk about to a doddering old man?" he would ask.

"Why don't you come along one day?" I replied, "he's such fun. . . and so knowledgeable. You know, he has a vast collection of books."

"I don't have time for a senile old man, and that, too, a stranger."

"He's old but not senile, not related to us, but not a stranger either. . . can't one make a stranger a friend?"

"Well, if you prefer old fogies for company, that's your problem," he said resignedly.

Even my friends wondered at my sudden and total withdrawal from their mid-morning coffee-cum-gossip sessions. I found them so puerile compared to my worldly wise, nimble-witted septuagenarian friend.

Visiting him and 'humouring' him — that's what my husband thought I did — in my spare time was bad enough, but not wanting to celebrate my birthday was unheard of. "You can't go into mourning just because that old man conked off," he objected. How could I explain to him that he was more than a mere old man... a friend, a mentor, a father, all rolled into one. Someone not easy to find or replace.

Our one year of friendship had taught me a lot, changed my very concept of life. How could I just discard those precious twelve months? The man had gone, but his words remained... words nobody had the time to listen to. Not even his own son.

I had sent him a telegram but there was no reply. Anxiously I waited. I had to hand over the house to its rightful owner.

I got a call from him after a week. He had been on vacation with his family and received the telegram only on his return. "When are you coming?" I asked. He seemed taken aback. "No point in coming now," he said tonelessly. "But the house..." I protested. "My lawyer will get in touch with you. Till then, please keep the keys with you."

The line got disconnected. The impersonal voice... did it really belong to his son? That he who throbbed with life and warmth could have such a child troubled me. Or maybe it was just the distance which made his voice sound so cold, so dead. So unlike the old man's, rich and vibrant. It still rang in my ears... strong and clear.

I could not keep away from the house. I could not let the plants wither. The lawyer had come and taken the keys. "What about the plants?" I blurted out. He had given me a strange look and walked away.

I took to watering the plants daily. They blossomed

under my tender care. My husband thought I had gone quite crazy. So did the neighbours who saw me tending the garden. "He's left the house to you?" one of them asked insinuatingly. "Maybe," I replied, tongue in cheek. After that nobody dared approach me, but tongues wagged. They wagged even more the day I had all the plants carted away to my house. I didn't care. That much I had imbibed from their owner.

And then, one day he arrived — the heir. To survey and evaluate his property, I suppose. What else could he have come for now, after a lapse of two years. He looked around at my blooming garden. "I want to thank you for looking after my father," he said solemnly.

"He needed no looking after," I replied, "we were just good friends."

He cleared his throat. "I believe you took away my father's plants after his death."

Stunned, I stared at him.

"I have bought a house... we plan to settle in India. My wife is very fond of gardening, and..."

Choking back my anger, I said, "You can have your, rather your father's, plants back. They belong to you."

"I wouldn't have asked... but you see, my wife..."

"It's alright," I said stonily, "they were not mine anyway."

"You can keep one or two if you like," he offered.

"No, thank you," I said, curbing the sudden urge to cry. "You can take them all."

He stood looking at my puckered face, then shrugged and said, "Thanks, anyway, thanks for looking after them," and walked away.

The Smothering

RITU BHATIA

THE SMUDGE OF dawn on the smoky night sky. A sleeping neighbourhood. Onto the window ledges and cracks in walls slither snowflakes, punctuating the blackened facades. Both sides of the road are lined with frosted cars. Mark unlocks a Buick and begins revving up the engine. Feet sunk in the iced pavement, Shashi keeps waiting. The tan coloured bumper disappears around the corner.

The apartment thaws Shashi. She turns on the television. "Bend, Stretch, Bend, Stretch!" Jane Fonda, bouncing up and down, a smile stapled to her face. Shashi's limbs, too, fly about in different directions. "You did it!" Jane shouts, 30 minutes later, throwing up her arms. Shashi turns on the percolator. Thoosh. Thoosh. The glass lid being knocked by the viscous liquid. A bitterness scalds her tongue. Black coffee and Jane Fonda are only some of Shashi's new habits. A nasal tone and chewing gum are others. She moves to the cot near the window. Kirk — the baby — is still asleep. All night long, Shashi has nursed him. But waking up at 5 a.m. to iron Mark's shirt and cook his egg sunny side up is as important. Mark is a tennis coach at the club and leaves early. Kicking, gurgling, Kirk opens his eyes; milky breath glides across his mother's face. She smiles and gathers the tepid body in her arms, flinging aside the tie-dye quilt her parents have sent for their grandson. Looking at the fabric brings back images of Shashi's mother: she'd be horrified to hear her grandson being called Kirk. . . How on earth does she expect anyone to call the baby Krishna? This is America. Why can't she be more tolerant, less horrified. . .

That she is a part of this new, rich country fills Shashi with pride. She can never thank Mark enough for giving her this opportunity. In the beginning, she worked at *Business Today*, a bi-monthly magazine, but quit when an American colleague, Samantha, less qualified and experienced than her, got the promotion she was expecting. But now, that's far behind. Nurturing Mark and his baby –– their baby –– is totally fulfilling. For a little pocket money, Shashi does flower arrangements at the florist's down the road. Her father, a professor of linguistics at Delhi University, would react violently if he knew. You, with your M. Phil in English literature, arranging flowers! What a waste! Don't you have any self-respect? What would our friends say? In India dignity of labour is non-existent. But then, in India, Shashi was considered privileged. Here she is like anyone else: an American. That suits her fine. A husband, a child, a home –– that's all she wants. That's all she ever wanted.

Their home –– a third floor apartment in Queens ––

is about the size of the drawing-room in her parents' Maharani Bagh house. Yellow walls covered with fading jonquils frame the single room. Squatting in its centre is a brown bed-sofa that remains a bed most of the day: Shashi spends a lot of time lounging on it, with Kirk. Watching the TV across. The women in the morning shows are especially interesting. Their lives are so complicated and exciting; ill-timed pregnancies and abortions, a new man every few months. A pile of newspapers and a pair of scissors lie on the ground. From them Shashi cuts out discount coupons: Save 25c on Pampers; 10c on Ivory soap. Meals are eaten on the laminated table in the corner. Cartons of old clothes, books, shoes, cluster together in nooks. One day, Shashi plans to donate these to Mother Teresa's charities.

Apart from the front door, there are two other doors in the apartment. One leading to the box-like kitchenette, the other to the bathroom. In her letter home, Shashi has written:

> We have a lovely apartment overlooking a park. Right now the lake has frozen and the trees are bare, stark as statues. Life here is great. I have lots to do, with Mark and Krishna. Though there have been many tempting job offers, I'm declining them until the baby is older. Last night we went to the Marlborough Music Festival and listened to Mozart's symphony no 41 in C major and Haydn's symphony no 94 in G major. The week before we were at the Fellini retrospective. Don't worry about me. I'm happier than I've ever been. . .

Through the slats of the only window, Shashi sees the street: narrow, lead-coloured, fringed by tall, frayed buildings. Wrought-iron fire-escapes run down their fronts, one on each floor. Policemen with dogs stalk the streets all day and night. Opposite, an old man in a vest watches television. The news makes him morose. So do commercials.

Shashi bathes Kirk, her attention on the screen. Mornings at home are usually quiet. No one calls or drops by. But Shashi doesn't need anyone. Kirk keeps her company all day. Kirk, Mark. . . they mean as much to her. Nobody else matters. Though Shashi does have a cousin -- Tara -- who lives off 5th Avenue, they don't meet often. Once in a while they talk on the phone: Tara advises Shashi on which store in the Little India block off Lexington sells the freshest okra. Their conversations often end with a rebuke from Tara: "When are you calling Mahesh and me over -- han? Mummy keeps asking about your apartment." On numerous occasions Tara has invited Shashi and Mark to dinner. Shashi has always declined: Mark is uncomfortable with other Indians. Also, Shashi does not want her life pried into. She had not given Tara their address: Indians have a notorious habit of dropping in without calling.

Kirk has had enough of the water. Carefully, Shashi wipes his arms and legs. Reaching for a Pamper, she finds the box empty. "Oh, hell!" This means a trip to the supermarket. Usually Mark and she shop together in the evenings: Shashi does not drive here. Lessons at Delhi's L-Star motor driving school have prepared her only for cluttered streets, chaotic, noisy traffic.

Automatic gears and smooth roads are too easy. She has nightmares about losing control; the car hurtling into a group of cows that stray suddenly onto an empty highway. . .

Besides, it's comfortable to let Mark do the steering. From her closet, Shashi pulls out a wind-cheater and some boots. Her only ornament, jangly earrings that disguise her as one of the Puerto Rican girls in the neighbourhood, swing at the base of her neck. Under the pram's wheels the warped stairs creak. An enormous woman unlocks a door on the second floor. She is enveloped by the stench of stale sweat. Averting her face -- the woman cleans others' houses for a living -- Shashi pushes the pram past. Except for a stray dog, the frozen streets are deserted. In summer the area brims with Cuban and Mexican teenagers, large, aggressive looking men in leather jackets and young girls arguing hysterically in Spanish. Everyone sprawls on the pavements; eating, drinking, smoking. Making love. Brawls are always taking place. Many nights, Shashi lies terrified, listening to the violent street noises, shouting, wails, the shattering of glass. Abused brakes and sirens. Once, even a gun shot.

A man walking a pomeranian ties it to the lamp-post outside Shop Rite. Inside, Shashi is greeted by colourful rows of everything a person could dream of eating. Shashi's letters to her mother still contain descriptions of stores and all that can be bought in America: juicy, luscious vegetables; sumptuous cheeses; milk with 4% fat, 2% fat and zero fat. Now, walking past glass cases filled with hams, hanging salamis, pink roast meat, Shashi remembers the times she accompanied her mother to Delhi's INA market. Behind the outer row of shops the inner alleys, crammed with tiny, brightly lit shops, their odours and colours blending to create a rich feast for the senses. The pickle shop: shrivelled mangoes and lemons exuding the smell of raw mustard oil. Yellows and greens and blacks of the grains in the grocery store. Down another alley, a row of utensil shops: metal saucepans, buckets dangling from shop fronts. Indolent shopkeepers hidden among all the pots and pans.

The poultry and fish section at the end of the market. Sodden ground: men, with cloths tied around their waists throwing pails of water outside their shops to wash away the remnants of freshly slaughtered chickens, or skinned fish. The powerful stench of fish and blood, raised stalls with men squatting behind blocks of ice strewn with limp chickens and portions of fish. On the ground, cages of squawking chickens. Knives being sharpened on a stone block. The shopkeeper's assistants hacking, skinning and weighing flesh dispassionately. Bargaining. A compromise and exchange of notes. Shashi's mother pleased that she had managed to save a few rupees.

Here, Shashi doesn't need to exchange a word with anyone while she shops. She just wheels a trolley around and keeps filling it with packets and tins. She goes past the cheeses and hams to the baby section. Kirk, who is sitting in the upper portion of the trolley, coos and reaches out to touch the packages. At the frozen food section, a group of dowdy Indian housewives touch and smell, discussing the merits and demerits of each packet in loud Gujarati. Turning her back to them, Shashi picks up a box of Pampers. But she has already been spotted; their voices drop, a conspiratorial tone. Shashi's face is hot: Indians in America are a real embarrassment, with their noisy, over-effusive manner; their habit of sticking together. A year ago, the Indian Association sent a representative with forms for her to fill. She refused.

"My husband is American," she told the tiny bespectacled man. He hadn't even argued. Shashi is amazed at how the Indians here always manage to recognise her; everyone else can't tell the difference between her and other dark-skinned American girls. Trying to avoid her countrymen is next to impossible. They turn up at the most unexpected places. It's almost nerve-racking. . . Walking out of Woolworth's the other day, Shashi was accosted by a ragged looking Sardar selling junk jewellery. "Sister," he began, tracing her steps, "Sister, please help me. . ."

Now that she has Kirk, their inquisitive looks have become insolent, sneering. But it doesn't matter to Shashi because lots of elderly American ladies stop and gush over Kirk: "Oh, honey, isn't he just gorgeous! Is he yours?"

Shashi holds Kirk even higher, "He sure is!"

That she has produced Kirk fills Shashi with awe. "You're mine. . . all mine!" she often whispers to him. Who thought mixed genes could result in such a fair, beautiful — American — baby. Why, his hair is almost as blond as his father's. He's just so much like Mark. . .

No one has ever depended upon Shashi the way her baby does, no one has ever trusted her so much. Kirk's feelings for Shashi are similar to her's for Mark. Shashi's parents, however, are disappointed with the photos she had sent home. "I wish Krishna had your eyes, or at least your hair. . ." her mother wrote.

A tapping and jangling as the cash register makes up her bill. Burly security guards watch from behind. Shashi's change is handed over. "Have a good day," says the girl at the register, looking above Shashi's head at the next customer.

At the apartment a letter from her mother awaits Shashi:

> Ram Bahadur has gone on leave for a week. I tell you, these wretched servants! One does so much for them and then they leave you with all the cooking to do. Anyway, the good news is that your father just won a prize for the double chrysanthemums he entered in the annual chrysanthemum show. Your cousin Alka is engaged. Her fiance, Anil Kumar, has an MBA from Wharton, owns a house in Sundar Nagar and has a membership at the Gymkhana Club. . .

At 4 pm, Shashi rocks Kirk to sleep and starts preparations for the evening. In the steaming, scented bathwater, she soaks. Her thighs redden as she pounds and pummels them under the water. This month's *Mademoiselle* says this helps reduce cellulite. Brooding, Shashi looks down at herself. Though regular workouts have improved her pear-shaped body, her legs are still stocky. In India, Shashi's figure was considered perfect; proportions designer made for sarees. But in America, a woman's image depends upon her legs. Visions of the supple, leggy girls Mark coaches appear like sudden flashes of light. Every time Shashi watches Mark play with one of them, she sweats: something about their overheated bodies, excess energy, stopped her visits to the club some months ago.

After checking that there are four cans of Lite beer in the freezer, Shashi takes out two rumps of meat and scrubs the potatoes. Cooking here is fairly simple; the elaborate dishes she learnt at Mrs. Bhatia's Cooking Academy in Delhi have long been forgotten. In fact, the greasy, overspiced foods of her childhood now upset her stomach.

Mark comes home late. It's become a habit lately. "Extra lessons, honey. . ." An apologetic expression. Walking straight to the TV he flicks it on and flings himself on the sofa. The sports commentator's voice fills the room. Shashi takes out a can of beer.

"Did you have a good day?"

Mark is absorbed by the football teams that have assembled at the centre of the field. "What? Oh, yeah... Sure. . ." Outside, it has stopped snowing.

Shashi sits beside Mark, tries to nuzzle up to him.

"Um. . . I'm kinda smelly, honey. . . maybe later. . ." Silently, they watch the ball game.

"You know, the Yankees are gonna beat the Brewers one day, that's for sure. . ." Mark's tone is confident. The camera shifts to the ecstatic crowd, all holding cans, packages of food, brightly coloured caps perched on their heads.

Shashi fetches a bowl of popcorn. "Hot, buttered. . . just the way you like it."

"Hey, thanks." Eyes rapt on the screen, Mark takes the bowl.

"Man, these guys are incredible." He rolls his eyes, shakes his head. "One day they're down, the next they're in good shape. . . it's really incredible. . ."

Shashi nods understandingly. Since Kirk was born, most evenings are spent watching TV, football mostly. Earlier, Shashi and Mark sometimes went disco dancing. The evenings she spent with friends in India — watching Sonal Mansingh dance, or listening to the filigree sounds of Hariprasad Chaurasia's flute — have long been forgotten. Shashi can't imagine how she could once reel off statistics on bonded labour in Bihar, or discuss India's economic future. Now, even reading is difficult. Not that it matters. Shashi's small cosy world — Mark, and their baby — keeps her happily occupied.

Shashi has left her hairbrush in the car. "I'm just going down, hons. . ."

"Oh, sure. . ." Mark doesn't even look at her.

A weeping sky. Below her Reeboks, iced ground. Blurred orange light splashes like exclamation marks through apartment windows. Shashi unlocks the car door, fingers stumbling on the wet metal. The smell of crushed potato chips clings to the upholstery. Shashi shifts to her own seat and opens the glove compartment. Under the papers, her hairbrush. She pulls it out and sits back, staring through the scarred windshield at blue streets; sniffing the perfume that's sticking to her seat. Musk? Patchouli oil? A thought that has been only faintly forming till now, begins assuming definition. Mark's been late the past few weeks. He's been so preoccupied, distracted. Such brief caresses. Could it be the short-haired blonde one? Maybe that tall, voluptuous one... Oh, no! No! No! Outside, Shashi takes deep gasping breaths, like an underwater swimmer surfacing for air.

Steak, the way Mark likes it — slightly underdone, with the pink still visible in the fibre — that's how Shashi cooks it. "Hey, this is great," Mark speaks through a full mouth. Whirling around from the stove, Shashi says, "You like it, really?"

"Sure, honey... didn't I tell you? It's great..." An arm around her waist, Mark puts his nose in Shashi's neck. She clenches her eyes, lips.

In a room saturated with darkness, Shashi gropes, emptying all Mark's pockets, smelling his clothes. The perfume is everywhere — it becomes more and more potent each moment. Numb, Shashi stands looking down at her sleeping baby, listening to the intimate grunts of pigeons on the ledge, struggling with a half-shaped resolve.

At dawn Shashi is awake. She irons Mark's shirt, fries his egg and goes down to see him off. A surly day. The snow has melted and brown slush smothers the pavements. All the bits of paper, plastic, cigarette wrappings hidden by the snow have reappeared. Strewn on the road is carelessly collected garbage; a mangled tin, vegetable peels.

On the TV Jane Fonda stretches and bends with her usual energy. Shashi doesn't. Instead she moves straight to Kirk's cot. The baby's trusting arms reach out. Shashi picks up the floppy body and presses it to her bosom.

"You sweetie pie, you angel, you. . ." Howls of protest ring out, but she does not loosen her hold. Shashi sinks her nose in his warm stomach with its talcum powder and mineral oil fragrance. Gently, she traces the pale scribbles on his palm. She then closes the blinds, and begins rummaging through the piles of T-shirts in her closet. At the bottom is an orange silk sari, worn by her to many Amjad Ali performances, in the hope that the vivacious colour would draw his eyes to her. Those evenings come back to her with a fearful clarity: the perfume of rose petals and marigolds strewn on the stage, the twanging sounds of the sarod, its sedative effect, the tranced, swaying audience. Standing before the mirror, Shashi drapes the sari around herself. The orange fabric billows about her, bringing back a face that has been forgotten. On her mouth and at the centre of her brows she smears red lipstick. She is graceful, elegant once again. The cherished daughter of Mr. and Mrs. Mehta. The Aroras' son, a banker with American Express, is listening to her views on V.S. Naipaul.

The apartment has darkened and shrivelled. Cold beads of sweat stand out on her forehead, crawl down her back. From the ceiling the sickly odour of wet nappies and milk hangs like a fog. Shashi notices coffee stains on the shaggy rug, the threads dangling from the sofa, the table, smeared with egg yolk and salt grains. She stumbles to the windowless kitchen. Cracked tiles stare at her. The skillet in which she had cooked the steak is heavy with congealed fat. In the brown-rimmed sink, unwashed cups and plates are jammed. Shashi places a panful of milk and water on the stove. To it she adds tea leaves, sugar, cardamom and cinnamon. A deepening colour. The masala tea turns amber. Shashi gulps it down, the stray tendrils of her hair curling in the perfumed steam. The sticky brew calms, soothes. Other occasions on which its magic has worked –– the chilly exam mornings, the day her grandfather died –– come back to her.

With Kirk on her lap, Shashi watches TV. A news flash cuts short the ecstatic expression of a woman with a bouffant who has won a washing-machine. A child molester is on the prowl. Parents are not to let their children out of sight; two children were murdered at a pizza parlour in downtown Manhattan. Kirk chuckles, squirms, kicks, but Shashi sits still. She is distracted by her baby's chubby legs; waxy, uncorroded skin. Closing her eyes, she tries to memorise it. Opposite, the old man has fallen asleep in his armchair. His head slumps woodenly on his chest, oblivious to the commercial advertising Sarah Lee poundcake.

Past Shashi, the ashen neighbourhood moves. A newspaper blows about in the breeze. In the gutter, an empty bottle rolls. People are huddled around fires: the aroma of fresh baked bread mingles with wood smoke. Shashi walks briskly, wheeling the pram past a black woman wearing a blond wig. The gray insular streets mock her: Did you really think we'd accept you that easily, they seem to say. Did you, did you, did you. . . Then suddenly they become crowded. People, cattle, cars, cyclists jostle about. Shashi's back in New

Delhi, in her father's car, gazing through the window at the street. An elderly woman is clambering on to a moving bus; moving dangerously close to a speeding car is a cyclist. A red light. A tattered child begs at the window, smudging the glass with her breath.

At Shop Rite Shashi searches frantically for the blowsy, homely figures of the Indian housewives. But today she is accosted only by the sterile rows, colourless vegetables. Not even the security guard looks her way.

The pram wheels squeak along until they reach a dead-end road. A junkyard. It is deserted at this time. Rusted metal, worn tires, sofas without legs, lie in piles. Still glowing are the remains of a fire. Snowflakes float in the air. Shashi settles the pram behind the piles, hidden from the road. She looks down at her baby. His innocent eyes blink in surprise as the furry grey puffs land on his face. He chuckles and tries to catch them. Shashi backs away, closing her ears to his confused cries. Snow is beginning to settle on the pram. Shudders run through Shashi; her eyes close. The family prayer room; the pictures of Lord Krishna become clear. Her senses are suffused by the sweet, woody fragrance of burning incense. Prayers for peace are being chanted by her mother, "Om Shanti Om, Om Shanti Om. . . ."

Shashi joins in. "Om Shanti Om, Om Shanti Om. . . Om. . . Om. . . Shanti Om. . ."

Rites of Passage

BULBUL SHARMA

'MANGALIK'. EVER SINCE I was a child this word had hung over me like a mysterious, frightening but distant threat. But I was not really afraid of it because I was not very sure what it meant. All I knew was that it was a terrible word and it belonged only to me. My mother would say it softly and sigh when she combed my long hair and plaited it each morning. I heard my grandmother hiss it out with anger every time I touched her special silver tumbler and even the servants often whispered it when I was in the kitchen and clicked their tongues in sympathy. Only my older brother thought it was a stupid word and got very angry when anyone called me 'Mangalik'. I knew he was jealous -- as usual -- of me. As I grew older I began to enjoy the special status the strange word gave me. I even liked its strange sound. The long soothing 'Mangal', a word my grandmother chanted the whole day and then the sharp, abrupt 'ik'.

What was it about this word, I wondered, but never asked anyone in case it was too frightening for me to bear. I wanted it to be a comfortable, familiar fear like the wicked old witch in the stories my grandmother told me or like thunder on a dark, rainy night. Then, when I turned fourteen the word was finally explained to me and it turned out to be a disappointment. All it meant, the priest explained, not to me but to my mother, was that the planets had not been moving in their proper order when I was born and my husband would die before me. I saw nothing terrible in this but my mother and my grandmother set up a wailing at once and even the maids joined in. Though the women had always known this is what 'mangalik' meant it was only when the priest pulled out his tattered red almanac and read out the exact time and date of my impending misfortune, that everything suddenly became official and my mother had to do something to mark the event. So she began beating her chest gently and crying.

After that was over, my father took charge. He called the priest into his study and shut the door on our curious faces like he always did when he entered that secret, forbidden room. As usual the women rushed to the window and sat down on the mat which was always kept there for them so that they could eavesdrop in comfort. The men began talking. The priest, an awkward young man, overcome by the honour of being allowed into the Raibahadur's special room, started stuttering and mumbling softly. We strained our ears to catch his words and my grandmother, who was slightly deaf, muttered angrily under her breath but did not dare curse him like she did when we mumbled. My father spoke loudly and clearly for our benefit because he hated repeating anything and he also wanted to finish the priest and my mother in one breath. "I am not a superstitious man as you know," he said looking at his bookshelf lined with heavy English journals and the priest too followed his gaze, muttering his ready agreement. "I do not believe in all this nonsense but what has to be done has to be done. I have read the scriptures from beginning to end and all the ancient sages say the same thing. The 'mangal grah' must be averted or else doom is certain."

The priest coughed once or twice to say that he too shared the same thoughts. "It is written that a girl who is a 'mangalik' is cursed to become a widow even after marrying a 'mangalik' boy, but another book says that there is a way to escape this."

Now the priest suddenly spoke up loudly. "I know... I know... marry her to a peepal tree."

My father did not like the way this important information was stolen from him and sat in stony silence for a while. The priest realised he had overstepped his brief and hung his head apologetically, in silence.

After a suitable pause to show his annoyance, my father began once more. "The girl is to be married to a peepal tree and then widowed. In this way the planets are fooled and the curse is averted."

The priest wanted to add many details to this curt information but he restrained himself. I could see him nodding his head and gulping down his rush of words.

"See to the arrangements and fix a date," said my father and went back to studying the new English journal which had just come for him from England that morning. The priest stumbled out of the room and was immediately engulfed by the women in a warm, eager, questioning circle. "What shall we do? You must tell us, Panditji. But first you must eat something," said my mother and guided him to our sitting room. The priest, regaining his dignity and importance quickly under my mother's kindly gaze, started talking clearly and confidently once again. In fact he began sounding a lot like my father.

"You will make arrangements for the wedding as soon as possible. All the rituals should be carried out properly, especially the widowhood otherwise the gods will not believe it has happened," he said, taking a small sip of the almond-flavoured milk my mother had placed before him. I will fix a date for the wedding after consulting the almanac. We will go to the riverside for the ceremony since the wedding and the widowing ceremonies can be performed there easily."

"Whatever you say, Panditji. Just rid my daughter of this 'grah'," said my mother with a deep, sorrowful sigh which, after years of practice, she had become very good at.

"Yes... yes. Do not worry," the priest replied, also looking solemn. But a tiny moustache of white foam covered his upper lip giving him the face of a sad clown and I could not help laughing. My mother slapped me gently like she does to show outsiders how strict she is with me and folded her hands in apology to the priest. After reluctantly accepting a small box of sweets and casting a quick look at the closed door of my father's study, the priest left. My mother and I at once broke into loud laughter but were quickly silenced by a gentle cough from the study.

From the next day my mother began preparing for my mock wedding. She ordered the munshi to buy bales of red silk, sequins and English satins and our old tailor was told to move into the small room along the verandah. I was measured a hundred times a day as my mother made the old man open the stitches and remake every garment. "Make it at least four inches bigger and then fold it. She can wear the same clothes for her real wedding. Why waste cloth?" she said, suddenly turning thrifty. But I was to have four new sets of gold ornaments though my mother had already made plenty of jewellery for me. She would often make me try on the glittering jewels and we both had a lot of fun doing this.

"This is a good time to get money out of your father. He will give readily now so why miss the chance?" she said, her eyes full of love and greed for me.

A dozen red and green glass bangles were bought too and my mother, for the first time, especially asked for the cheap thin ones. "They have to be broken. The expensive ones will take a long time and your father is sure to get angry." She also bought one cheap white sari for me to wear when I was widowed but for some reason she kept it bundled up in one corner and would not let me look at it. She kept ordering little things like silver boxes for sindoor, mehndi, red ribbons, and gold buttons every day and the poor munshi rushed in and out of the house with her lists.

Everyone in the house was infected by my mother's enthusiasm and her frantic preparations and even my father stopped by on his way out one day to see what the tailor was doing and made him spoil an entire row of stitches! Only my brother kept muttering that all this was a load of rubbish and we were behaving like illiterate people, but since he never had the courage to protest in front of my father, the only literate person beside him, we did not care what he thought of us or my impending wedding. My grandmother too was angry about my mock wedding to the peepal tree but for a different reason. She did not like the way my mother was enjoying herself preparing for the event.

"First she gives birth to three dead sons and only one live one. Then she produces one girl and that too a 'mangalik'. Now she is fleecing my son to have jewels made for herself," she said to the maids every morning when they cleaned her prayer room. She shut her eyes and clutched her prayer beads in her fist angrily whenever she saw me now.

"You think the gods can be fooled so easily? They can see what is going on. They can look down and see that a four-inch hem has been left on the girl's kurta. They will know at once she is neither a real bride nor a widow," she told my mother every day.

But as usual my mother ignored her. She made a pile of new clothes not only for me but for herself as well. She bought a silk kurta for my father and one for my brother, but he threw it back at her and said, "I don't want to participate in this mumbo jumbo. How can my father, an educated man, allow you to do this to the poor girl? All of you think it is a game, a doll's wedding. . ." My mother just laughed and pulled his hair and he walked off angrily. The next day he went back to his college even though he still had a few days of holiday left. I was happy he had gone. He was no fun these days, though I liked the word 'mumbo jumbo' that he kept saying all the time.

Three days before my wedding a halvai was called to set up a temporary kitchen in the courtyard and great cauldrons full of delicious smelling food bubbled and steamed all day. Though no relatives were invited for the event (we were under strict intructions from my father not to tell anyone about my planned wedding to the peepal tree), my mother's family, who lived in the same town as us, began to have all their meals at our home. My grandmother would watch from her window as they arrived promptly at mealtimes and abuse them softly. They could not hear her and would turn their happy faces to her window and fold their hands respectfully. How much I used to laugh then!

My father, after giving his consent, maintained an aloof silence as usual but my mother took care to keep the activities away from his part of the house and made sure her relatives did not stray anywhere near his study. Then, finally, the day of my wedding arrived. I was made to bathe early in the morning but only after my mother had rubbed a paste of turmeric and sandalwood powder on my body. "There is no need to do all this but why not have a proper rehearsal for your wedding?" she said, laughing, and hugged me. She now no longer sighed when she combed my hair though she still called me 'mangalik' in a funny, teasing way.

On the day of my wedding the entire household got into three tongas very early in the morning and after some confusion and delay because the priest had sat down next to the cook by mistake and in the process also squashed the huge ball of dough meant for the puris, we finally left the house. All along the way, the priest kept checking his new dhoti which bore a damp moon-shaped stain on it now. "Do you think I should bathe before the ceremony?" he asked my grandmother.

"You can bathe a hundred times in the Ganga but you cannot fool the gods," she said, pointing to the sky. The priest thought she was talking about the puri dough and got even more nervous. He sat with his head bent for the rest of the journey. Was this a bad omen too — like so many others that took place that morning? Afterwards, my mother tried to recall those signs many times. "What happened had nothing to do with anything that was done or not done by you," my brother would say but she never believed him and neither did I. The priest, the planets, the gods, the peepal tree — everyone seemed to have plotted against me that day.

But when we reached the river that morning the sun shone like a gold and silver disc and everything, the river, the trees, the flowers looked so fresh, happy and beautiful. They were to betray me later, but today they beamed and smiled kindly. The sky was a strange pink, tinged with grey and gold, a colour I had never seen before, but then I had never got up this early in the morning and I kept yawning all the time. My new red silk dupatta did not look as pretty in the morning light as it had done at home and I wanted to take it off. But my grandmother tied it tightly around my waist and told me sharply to sit down in one place. "At your age I was married for two years already and not a wild lamb like your mother has made you," she said, but then suddenly patted my cheeks. "Remember to give that new white sari to me. Don't put any marks on it. I will give you halva at home," she said, smiling sweetly, just the way she did when I tickled her feet or when my father scolded my mother.

My mother was busy arranging all the puja things we had brought for the priest and my father sat far away under a large umbrella held by a servant boy. It looked as if he had not come with us at all and was a stranger, but for once he was not reading his English books. Though it was still early morning, it was beginning to get hot now and he asked the priest to hurry up with the ceremony. But there seemed to be some argument about which peepal tree to choose. My mother wanted the tall sturdy one with a dense crown of leaves but the priest had already selected a slender young one with branches.

"What does it matter? Just get on with the ceremony," said my father irritably.

My mother had to obey him but she grumbled softly to me all the time as she poured ghee into the havan. "Now I am sure my son-in-law will be a sickly, thin boy. Why could we not choose the stronger tree? See how shiny and dense its leaves are! Just like your father's hair when I married him."

The priest ignored her and carried on chanting but my father cleared his throat in a reprimanding tone and silenced her. The sun had now reached high up in the sky and all the lovely colours of the morning had vanished. The priest droned on till he was ordered by my father to shorten the ceremony and he quickly finished it off with one hastily mumbled prayer. Then he began preparing for the widowhood rituals. The peepal tree's pale grey trunk was smeared with turmeric and ghee and then, after a dramatic pause, the tree — my bridegroom — was cremated with a burning twig. The smoke began to hurt my eyes as the priest started his mournful chanting once more and I burst into tears. My mother laughed and said "Oh the poor thing is feeling sad about losing her husband!" And even my father twisted his face into a thin smile. But the priest did not like my wailing and hurried on with his prayers.

"It is not a good omen," said my grandmother as she walked up to us. She had been sitting far away under the shade of the peepal tree my mother had wanted me to marry because, being a real widow, she could not attend my wedding. Now that I had been widowed she could come and sit with us. She pushed my mother away and took charge. "Fetch a big stone. First break her bangles and then wipe the sindoor off. Cut her hair a few inches," she barked at the maids.

But my mother would not let her touch me. "Let us go and eat first. Otherwise all the delicious food we've brought with us for the wedding feast will be spoilt." She ordered the servants to bring the food out and told the cook to heat the oil for the puris.

"It is too late now, you should have eaten before I started the last rites," said the priest who had by now turned into an enemy.

"Never mind, we can treat it like a shraddha and still eat," answered my mother who always won every argument she started except the ones with my father.

The food was quicky brought out by the servants who were as eager to eat as us and before my grandmother and the priest could appeal to my father the cook, who had kept everything ready, began frying the puris. The aroma of pure ghee floated out onto the clean river air and the priest succumbed at once with a feeble, "the brahmin has to be fed in any case."

After we had eaten and the servants had cleared the dishes the widowing rituals began. Just to annoy my grandmother my mother told me to first take my bridal clothes off. The maids held up two sheets and made a tent. My mother slipped the red kurta, now crumpled and sweaty, over my head carefully and folded it. "You have dropped kheer on it, you silly girl," she said but she was not angry. Her beautiful face shone with excitement and I could see that she was quite happy. She took all my jewellery off and made me wear the white sari. It was cooler than the silky bridal clothes but it felt strange. I had never worn a sari before and had trouble walking out of the tent. But when I came stumbling out, no one spoke or laughed and suddenly the happy day became different.

The servants watched with suspicion and fear in their eyes as my grandmother broke my bangles on a stone, and my mother was quiet for the first time that morning. We now sat by the river in a huddle under the larger peepal tree and no one seemed to know what to do next. Long shadows stretched on the river and flies buzzed around my face. The priest too was not sure how long this mourning period should last and watched the cloudless sky as if to ask its advice.

"They are watching," whispered my grandmother and I thought she was talking about the urchins who had gathered to eat the scraps. "From heaven, they are watching. It is not so easy to fool them," she repeated a little louder this time, and my mother, surprisingly, did not answer her back. The sun was now high above our heads and a hot, dusty breeze blew around us. My red bridal dupatta unfolded itself from the neat pile and fluttered in the wind. My head ached and I wanted to go home. I whined softly to my mother and she patted my head. "It is over now. We will go home and you will have lots of sweets and dozens of new red and green bangles."

But that did not happen. The gods were not fooled. I was married the following year. My husband who, strangely enough, looked a lot like the thin grey, peepal tree, died within three months of my wedding. I never wore red bangles again but no one in my family called me a 'mangalik' anymore. They did not call me anything at all.

Dying Like Flies

RUCHIRA MUKERJEE

SENIOR CIVIL SERVANT shoots himself. A three-inch column in the Saturday morning paper, front-page news. A Joint Secretary in the Ministry of Defence is found locked in his study Friday night, a bullet in his temple. There follows a list of important posts held, past tense. I am my limbs, and then this shroud, and then the silken rope binding me to a frail bed that is carried swaying, rhythmical, to the graveyard... And then the wicked coffin and the dark, cool, narrow bed they place it in, and the fragrant, freshly dug earth falling, falling. I am softly, lovingly encased with all who went before me.

Salim Farooqui, born a Muslim, was not religious and would have liked (since rites were inevitable) a silent, inconspicuous burial. They came for the funeral in scores, wordless men in white caps, curious, stumbling over uneven soil. A stunned wife and two sons (who could make neither head nor tail of the whole thing) were questioned briefly. Was he murdered? He had, murmured friends, not an enemy in the world.

Suicide then? It was definitely suicide. Farooqui had signed certain arms' deals — had a 'foreign power' twisted his arm too far. . .? Or was it that he'd slipped up in his youth (the days of relative obscurity) in a matter affective or pecuniary, and the past now reared its ugly head in the shape of a blackmailer. . .? May be. . . Two Britons on Janpath at mid-day had their own explanation. "It's the 'eat gets everybody finally, addles the brain, turning 'em poor folk to unnatural acts. A glance at the newspaper tells you. . . there they are, dying like flies." About one thing they were entirely right — it was June, and the hottest week of the year. Not a very good time to be alive.

Friday evening had brought to an end hours of dullness on the new missile. Rates, discounts, time of delivery. . . His eye rested on the desk's green felt, letting a soft, mossy emptiness into his beleaguered brain. The voices of two Joint Secretaries came across the partition, thickening the air with portent.

"When I entered", said Sinha, "Secretary was speaking of the French product, its reliability, the trial runs. . . All the while, the Prime Minister sat reading a file. In the end, she raised her head and said: 'Well, that's that, gentlemen. Any comments on quality, the scientific levels? Salim, do I see disapproval on your face? Don't just sit there, tell us something.' "

"You sure?" said Verma, in disgust and awe. "Such bad form to check with a junior. . ."

"The man to see was Farooqui," said Sinha, silencing him. "He closed the file and shut his eyes like the Buddha, a full minute. Clause by clause, he then demolished the case put up by the Secretary. All the technologies on offer were antediluvian, he said, the nerve of the man. . . It was decided to float the tender again. Secretary is furious."

Farooqui swivelled his chair round once fully suppressing an oath of delight. Of course, he's furious. . right dull these meetings get.

"Mind you," said Sinha "bad things don't happen to people like Farooqui. They always fall on their feet."

"So would you," retorted Verma, "if you had connections in high places. Then you'd have gone about with that marvellous air of not caring. Of treating life humorously."

"Oddly," said Sinha after a moment, "Farooqui really doesn't care. . . I've a feeling he'd just smile if he were passed up for Additional Secretary."

"But he won't be, don't you see? These people lead a charmed life. Farooqui's father is royalty, State of Loharu, who sent his son to Doon and Oxford. . . Salim Farooqui took a first in Philosophy and married Sir Qaiser Mohammad's daughter. He has two sons now, both strong and clever. The wife is a bit. . . snobbish, and expensive to support, but Farooqui's family has such wealth that, for two generations, nobody need go to work, yet eat biryani and dress in brocade. . ."

"Personally," murmured Sinha, "I'd say Farooqui's a good egg, generous, keeps himself to himself. . . and such pleasant manners. It's just that he's got it all laid on while you and I scramble for scraps all our lives."

Salim Farooqui stared at the paperweights on his desk, their icy blue-green flame. Verma and Sinha were dead right. His wife was so beautiful, it gave you a shock looking at her, his father loved him to distraction. . . and he'd never failed at anything himself, had he? Yet before each major event he had thought, what emptiness, what flat beer, surely there's more to things. . . There'd been pleasures, keen and variegated, but each time an aftertaste had come, tobacco on the tongue, the question: is that all? Life (when good) yielded humour, as people did with their cupidity and bad taste, their absurd seriousness. . . The bad times brought a deadly boredom to chore and pleasure alike, he found folks around him repugnant on those days, he found himself disgusting. Somewhere, he incoherently felt, life had a responsibility for filling up an inner space which didn't yet have a name. You didn't think about it, of course, better to do files or play a game of tennis. . . Yet, plop in the middle of a warm, slow patch in the music, the sound of thunder or the crickets' morse, there it was, a stir and the fine, lurching hope. He would wait. . .

He worried his memory for the good times, his qualifying for the Civil Service. His tiny, octogenarian grandmother rocking back and forth on paan-stained sheets, singing to him her toothless, quavering song of congratulation. The women servants had come one by one to crack their knuckles at his temple and ward off the evil eye. Venison, and Abba asking him up for their first drink together. Salim had seen unfurl in the golden water a life of trivial responsibility. . . I have done what people wanted of me. . . all I wanted was to play the violin, and stir the sleeping chords in restless men. . . After a meeting with the Prime Minister now, he would slip silently to stand (lean, greying ghost) behind a great padded chair in his room, addressing empty sofas before him. . . Gentlemen, lest you forget, the business we deal in is war . . . the country's splendid plan to kill people like us in other countries. . . He hoped by the melodrama to diminish sensation, the boredom and the fright of an infant before a giant, coal-black cloud as he opens with morning radiance the balcony door.

Sayeeda Zaheer, Deputy Secretary, entered his office. No staff cars were available for bringing a Swedish delegation in from the airport. All taken, she seethed, by the Minister's personal staff. A prim little manager Sayeeda was, beneath the startled, willowy exterior. Salim found her both comical and touching in these moods.

"Not the Day of Judgement yet, Sayeeda," he quipped in a teasing Urdu. "Must you take it all so hard?"

"Not as annoying," she replied in English, "as people who can't be made to take anything seriously."

A tune shoots swiftly through his head in a diving, stairlike sequence — Mozart, but which symphony? Sayeeda rises to leave, it isn't right to offend her, we've worked together many years. . . She accepts, reluctantly, a fizzy drink and her collarbone is slender ivory as in girls at puberty, a light down darkening the forearm. Farooqui makes three calls, soft, peremptory, and it's all arranged. A car to meet the Swedes, lunch next afternoon at a prominent hotel, an appointment with the Defence Minister. He laughs under his breath.

"What is it amuses you?" scolded Sayeeda, relieved.

"That you try so hard, your agitation. Why does it matter so much, the business of failing? Fail if you must."

"You wouldn't like that, I can tell you," said Sayeeda quietly. "You go to town as soon as people about you begin to take it easy."

"Are you saying that I'm difficult to work for?"

"Damnably," she replied, dimpling deeply at the impudence.

He felt a tightening in his chest, a motor-car accelerating to crazy speeds inside the skull. She must in no event be allowed to leave the room. . . something urgent he had to find out this evening, something she must be made to say. Behind the motor-car was the lambent tune from Mozart, maddening in its familiarity, flickering and nameless.

Krishnan, under secretary, entered with a sheaf of letters to be signed. "Off you go then, Sayeeda," said Farooqui, vanquished. "Have a nice weekend." He stared in mock horror at the pile of correspondence before him, clapping a clown's hand to his eyes. "You're invited to breakfast tomorrow, Krishnan. These should be ready about then."

Salim Farooqui lay on white satin cushions in the living room. His sons were away and their mother came yawning into the room, which shrank but acquired a gilt edge, to dial her parents' number. She was accustomed to spending whole days worrying the little instrument, calling friends, her confectioner, making appointments for a hair-set or manicure. Tall and striking in appearance, her eyes were always the untroubled turquoise of a swimming pool through the water. Firoza.

"Hello, Ammi. Are the boys okay? Don't give them pudding for dinner, the older one gets pimples. And Hanif has to be taken for a filling. . . Salim? He's back early for a change. Brought work home with him, of course, something for the Prime Minister. . . He's wearing the lovely mulmul kurta you sent. . . Yes, okay. Valeikum salaam, Ammi."

She curls up, freshly bathed, on the carpet beside Salim and a keen summer scent assails his nose. Khus. I don't like my work, he wants to say, I want a change to Industry or Home Affairs. We keep planning here for grisly wars, squandering criminal sums. . . But darling, Firoza will pout, you wouldn't be so important elsewhere, so much in the eye of the. . . Success counts with Firoza.

"You start to read as soon as you get home," she says, laying her cheek upon his breast, "Firoza feel very lonely. Salim no kiss Firoza."

He strokes her hair, watching the old familiar things tonight for traits of ugliness, of dissonance. A phone rings and here's Firoza, swiftly gathering up her swirling satins, and there's Firoza, darting across a polished floor. . . Two evenings ago, they had swerved upon a moonless road, the headlights of a facing car upon them, and her lips had drawn nervously back over long, white teeth. When she pressed the accelerator, an autumn mane had fanned up behind her head (as she galloped, drunk upon the wind), a faultless rhythm governing her knees and haunches. . . As she speaks on the telephone, a glowing neck arched, jerking her lean cheek this way and that, a rich neighing fills the room. Her-her, goes her deep-chested laugh, her-her-her-her. A hesitant hoof at the forelock, and here she comes, cantering, leggy, towards the sofa. Salim sits up in alarm, his forehead covered in moisture. Firoza hands him a tall beer and (seeing her widened eyes, the hair's nubile lustre) it is all as before. . . even the slack mouth, her witless look.

"Phuphi is arriving from the States tomorrow. She'll fall out of the car when she sees Hanif. He looks exactly like Abbu did at that age, I'm told."

Phuphi and Abbu, Salim catches himself thinking, and before long, Khala and Abbu and Ammi. What if, just for once, Firoza comes up with something really interesting. About the world, children, anything, only, please God, not her family.

"Let's go to the hills for a week," says Firoza, taking a sip out of his glass. Wet lips and lightly mussed hair. "Ammi will keep the boys."

Salim's throat tightens with a fear that is difficult to dispel this evening. Why would he want to be alone with his wife, what will he say to her? She hums in a small, toneless voice a Sixties' film tune, and the snaking afternoon symphony is falteringly reborn.

"What's that tune?" he says, alert.

"Talat Mahmood. *Don't let your love for me increase/ I am a shiftless cloud. What has he on offer/Who owns no roof, no pride.*"

But the tune, where did that come from?

Firoza asks the bearer for ice and there it is again, a hard-hoofed stamping and a vein standing out in her temple. Perhaps I no longer love her, thinks Salim. She has turned to face him, and is again his ingenuous bride, saying, don't you agree?

"Yes," says Salim, "yes." You can't disagree with Firoza, she always has the right intention.

At dinner, Firoza calls the cook kambakht, good-for-nothing (the koftas are cold) and a small, blinding wick lights up between his eyes as he clasps his wife's hand, despairing, to his breast. It feels as if he's never been in love with her at all.

Firoza is leaving for a Marilyn Monroe film, will he come? I've a brief to do, says Salim, kissing her forehead. For the Prime Minister... With a drumming in the head and nerveless, clammy palms, Salim goes out to the bristling grass before the house. For air, night sounds, the ill-paid watchman ringing listlessly an enervated hour. And, not least, to banish by the fresh heat's slap the spectres that crowd his brain tonight. Before he can approach the files waiting in his study...

He removed his slippers on the grass. Above and around, encasing him in a motionless, steaming jar was the shocked June night. (He thought of other nights, and under his feet, the tickling, dirtying, irrepressible dew...) He would ask Sayeeda to arrange a typist for tomorrow. Had she made arrangements for the conference, its venue, minutes...? Sayeeda, always Sayeeda, he needed another Deputy Secretary... She was good and wise, of course, a bit of a prig, but frank. Brutally frank. There swam before him two small craters a childhood pock had left beside her clear eye, his face growing warm with tenderness. You couldn't call her beautiful, too grave her face was for that, and in recent times, in a bad temper.

Was he... in love with her? Sayeeda had been on holiday once, a whole month. He had been annoyed beyond endurance by her ageing replacement, his listening without demur, the long, toneless notes in a microscopic hand. Till, unexpectedly, with the budget still in session, Sayeeda had returned to work, her skin aglow... Salim felt a dull distress, a swift loss of pleasure. It had been Sayeeda all the time. What was he doing, the girl just thirty-two, he at least twenty years older... He tried to recall with desperation the face he saw each morning in the shaving mirror. Ascetic, hair more white than black, long vertical lines in the cheek. In the eyes, a hooded hauteur.

There sounded footsteps on the gravel beyond the hedge, Sayeeda walking her dog. Barefoot, he flew to the gate.

"Miss Zaheer... I say, Sayeeda."

She turned, startled. She'd been years in the neighbourhood, never once had the reticent Farooqui interrupted her brooding, after-dinner walk.

"I wonder," said he, "if I may get your p.a. to type something tomorrow morning? I've an urgent brief to get off."

"Let's see... I think I can arrange something. Nayar. Bumptious, but excellent typing. He'll be with you by nine, is that okay?"

"Perfect."

No more to say, and both stood rooted, unable to move. Sayeeda's hair was open down to the waist, the street lamps casting strange shadows about her face. She looked mysterious, older somehow, her kurta of the same gauzy, flowing white as the one on the man before her.

"You look different," he heard himself remark. And felt at once angry and sickened by the certainty of failure in saying what he had to.

"I've washed my hair," she replied.

Salim heard himself describe (easily, naturally) the conversation of the Joint Secretaries, Verma and Sinha, their verdict upon him. He spoke of a disenchantment with his job, he had wanted to play the violin. . . Born, of course, with the old silver spoon, but disappointed with his discovery of what life contained. And flecked with a powdery guilt at all times about feeling that way. . . He wanted Sayeeda to say that he had had a wonderful life, that she envied him. Sayeeda stood motionless as the glistening neem on that still, burning night, the dog temporarily forgotten.

"Aren't you going to tell me what you think?" he said in the end. "Do you indict me, too, for my good fortune and the levity I meet it with at every turn ?"

She was silent still.

"Speak," he urged.

"I'm at a loss," said Sayeeda, struggling between charity and the truth. "I don't believe that pleasures or quick success ever gave real satisfaction. What is the joy to an infant who is born a king?"

"I don't understand," said Salim, confused. "Don't you agree that there stands before you an uncommonly lucky man?"

"No, Sir. I think that you possess bright things, numerous things, and live in a sort of cocoon. Safe from the problems that besiege existence, the big questions. . . I do not think what you have enhances the quality of your life."

"In what," he smiled sardonically, palms sweating, "is happiness to be found?"

"That's easy," she replied, her voice growing softer. "In the simple things. In learning and landscape, in squeezing every brain or body cell, doing the thing for which one was intended, one's avocation. . . ? Then, sharing the day's chores, its humour and secrets, with the person one loves. . . And, most important, in wanting something deeply, crazily, in working towards the dream, and, little by entrancing little, in seeing it happen one day before one's eyes."

It was Salim's turn to be silent. After a while, he gruffly asked, "And has life been kind to you in all these ways?"

She gave no reply, only a shadow, pain probably, crossed her eyes before she began looking for the dog. Salim was filled with tenderness, wrenching and like the sea. We're of a kind, aren't we, he wanted to say. He said instead with uncharacteristic boldness, "I don't know how it's said, Sayeeda, but I've a special feeling for you in recent times. . . It's like I neither see nor fully understand the things I meet, books, people, terms of contract. . . until I have first shown them to you. Before that, I'm restless. . . do I make sense? You won't have guessed after all. . ."

"I've noticed," she admitted, artless, gentle.

He was shocked, whatever gave her the idea? "How long have you known then?"

"Roughly over a year," she replied, without a trace of self-satisfaction.

It plunged him into a series of dark thoughts, no fool like an old fool, she's had me at her mercy. "Does it disturb you," he asked, "this emotion for which I feel in no way responsible?"

"No," she replied, smiling. "Your conduct has been irreproachable."

After a silence: "Had the circumstances allowed, Sayeeda, and had I asked, would you have joined your life with mine?"

"I would have, Sir."

"Sir," he laughed (it seemed at himself) under his breath. "I wanted to say. . . will you look in on the boys sometimes? They are growing up silly, a little out of touch. . . Somebody needs to talk to them."

Sayeeda hesitated, but the desperation in his eyes forced her. "I will, Sir," she said slowly.

"Right. Maybe you should turn in now, get a good night's rest. . . Here's the old mongrel, bad boy," said Salim, bending to pat a huge, importunate labrador that had bounded into their pale flickerings with a black and quickened life.

He walked briskly indoors, an exultation, silent, uncontainable, exploding his cranium. She loves me, she loves. . . It was, it seemed to him, the moment, glittering and uncorrupted as a diamond, for which all past years had been a preparation. He no longer felt amused. . . something was required of him (large, ambitious) ripping the shimmering tinsel of his days down the centre. A terrible thumping filled his chest, leaving his body both tired and unbearably excited. . . a stone released by a catapult, hurtling into an impossible sky. He tried to calm himself. If my breathing slows down, and I get my limbs to obey, all of this will settle before long into a gemlike clarity, the next thing to be done. . . In fact, he wished to do nothing. It pealed inside (the joy), giant church bells in a small, forgotten village, long and deep and deafening. . . I knew not of the existence of this, the madness, the wonder. . .

Firoza was not home. Salim bolted the front door, and checking for loitering servants in the downstairs rooms, entered his study. He looked once round, a swift counting up, a locking into doomed memory, and switched off the only lamp that lit his path. He felt his way to a favourite armchair, its fading upholstery, and rested his head a moment on the cushioned back, unwinding as for a night's sleep. He thought of Sinha's face, puffy from drink and incomprehension at the office next morning, and smiled. He drew out then from a drawer in the writing table, a small, heavy pistol, smelling of an innocent grease. There came to him, fortissimo, the day's ranging, stairlike melody, complete this time with its name. The fortieth symphony of Mozart in D minor, one of the first pieces he had heard as a child. He wished Sayeeda could hear his recording of the London Philharmonic and have the waves burst upon her, huge, grey-green, smothering, as they did upon him now. He checked (with dry, narrow fingers) the pistol for cartridges, and pushed the drawer tidily into place.

The heat had entered the bowels of the city. It pierced your back through the mattress, and enveloped you in a tight coat of steam if you went for an evening walk. Food was abhorrent, and no desert cooler could slake the ugly, burning ball of anger that rested its elbow inside you. About Salim Farooqui, the whispering went on for a while, he had near relatives in a country with whom India had gone to war. . . Sinha became Additional Secretary, and even caught before he retired (for an insignificant act of loyalty) the eye of the Prime Minister. It was noticed at once by his colleagues who, ambitious and dull as himself, forgave him in the end. The man they did not forgive was Salim Farooqui who, having wrung from life her rare and most precious gift, spat in her eye and was content to lie in the deep, brown mud amidst beetles and surging roots, the keen, coursing moisture and dead dreams. A very cool place, with no outlets.

The Manuscript

DEEP BEDI

THE TRAIN MOVED into the station, the brakes made their indeterminate sound as it slid along the platform and stopped with a loud sigh. Passengers began packing their luggage; bed rolls, tin boxes, food baskets, water containers. The journey had come to an end. The compartment was littered with peanuts, banana peel and bits of paper, remnants of a long and tedious journey. The acrid smell of uneaten food was overpowering. And my fellow passengers smelt no better. Three days of being confined in that little space had left us bedraggled, the wooden seats had rendered harsh treatment to our backs and our bones creaked and protested like the brakes.

Porters wearing red shirts and white dhotis rushed into the compartment. The crowd jostled and pushed outwards: elbows accidentally poking stomachs while tin boxes found their way onto heads. I remembered to keep my cool and follow the normal procedure; check the porter's number and then the baggage. I left the compartment, covered with dust and soot and began to make my way to the taxi stand of the Maurya Nagar station.

The station was like any other except for the building. The structure was impressive and reminded me of the British Raj. Constructed with brick and mortar and painted deep yellow with red stripes across, it was attractive and cleaner than the north Indian stations to which I was accustomed. A delicious aroma of South Indian coffee, dosas and vadas hung in the air — fresh coffee beans have a different flavour. The people were different too. No tall, stalwart Sikhs with beards, no fair women in salwar kameez. Dark, short men wearing dhotis, affluent dark women wearing diamond noserings; the poor with cane baskets balanced on their heads hurrying into already overcrowded compartments. I came out of the station to see a large enclosure filled with taxis, autorickshaws and horse carriages.

I was here at last! Why this nostalgia? Why these vibrations, and then sudden peace? I stood taking it all in. My restlessness had vanished. I had reached my Mecca. Why hadn't I come here earlier? She had asked me to. Now I was seeing it through her eyes. I became aware of the clamour of human voices. "Sahib, tonga sahib. Taxi Mister. It will take you right to top of hill. Very good place. You see the city from there. It look very good. Maharaja palace very good."

I have never stopped wondering why a tourist seems to be marked with an invisible badge. Yes, I did have to go to a place near the palace. To Kismet to be precise. I had to find her manuscript, the one I had not accepted many years ago. I wanted to relive her life, her agony, her joy and her passions.

Before I could choose a taxi, I saw, to my consternation, that my luggage was already neatly stacked in the boot of one. I smiled and nodded my approval to the taxi-driver. He was a talkative chap.

"Maurya Nagar very good place sir," he said, starting the car. "You will like it. I will tell you all the places to see sir. Sir museum very big, sir. Beautiful paintings of King Tipu and the British General, even our Maharaja, but not this Maharaja, many years ago." He laughed at his own joke.

As the taxi sped along the broad, clean roads I was content to listen to him.

"On the right is Government Hospital." I saw the building which must have been the Maharaja's palace at one time.

"On the left is the Exhibition Gallery, over there the handicraft centre and that. . ."

I stopped listening to my self-appointed guide. The taxi was ancient and couldn't have been moving at more than eighteen miles an hour. I looked through the window which offered me a panoramic view of the city. A city with character. I discovered that the monarch was a lover of beauty. The buildings didn't look unkempt, nor were there innumerable colours to distract the onlooker. They were all painted yellow. The main street was broad and the footpaths were bordered with iron railings.

"The statue is of our present Maharaja and to the left is his palace." It was an enormous palace: the blue and orange hues of dusk enhanced its splendour.

"You must come here in Dusserah. Very big festival

in October. Many people in villages come and many white people too. Maharaja sit on elephant. Elephant wear gold jewellery. Maharaja also, and both go in big procession. At night the palace lighted with bulbs. Look very nice. But the Congress Government give no money. Maharaja also not so rich. When I was young the festival very good, not so good now."

I was amused. He obviously missed the splendour of the feudal age.

I was nearly at my destination. I could feel it. Cool avenues with trees on either side, flowers with their colour heightened by the inky blue dusk of the setting sun. She had loved these flowers and the lakefuls of lotus. She had loved the picturesque serenity and the people of Kismet. There was the hill! The temple at the top was like a sentinel, she had said. The pretentious sentinel. Her faith had been destroyed gradually by humanity, monuments and idols. Who am I to condemn a place of worship? I failed her as a human being.

More trees, like she had said, cool and soothing. The orange and red flowers danced in the breeze. We were approaching Kismet. I could see it in my mind's eye. And there it was, hidden behind the Gulmohar and the jacaranda! I could see Kismet in the bright moonlight. The gate was closed. The house looked abandoned.

"You want to go to the hill now, the city look very nice from top." The taxi driver was tired after the long drive.

"No I want to go to the Palace Hotel."

"The new big hotel, there it is; very good place."

The drive to the portico was a long one. On the right

were fields, silvered in the moonlight. On the left, well maintained lawns and fountains. The taxi stopped in the portico. My luggage was taken out by a porter. I walked to the reception and inquired about my reservation.

"Your name, Sir?"

"Vijay Mehta."

"Yes sir, we have your telegram. Here is the key, Room 101." He gave me the register to sign.

"How long do you plan to stay, sir?"

"Two to three weeks perhaps."

"Not many tourists at this time," commented the receptionist.

"Oh, that's all right. I will be happy here, I need the rest." I looked out of the lobby window and breathed deeply.

"Doesn't anyone live in that house?"

He was willing to provide the information.

"No sir, there was a family living there once but they all scattered in different places. Drink and women. . ."

"I want to see the place," I cut him short.

"An old retainer lives there alone. I am sure he can show you around."

I took my key and went to my room to freshen up. I couldn't visit Dru covered with dust. The house may have been neglected but to be with Dru, I had to be clean. I wanted to see her home at night. All the senses are at their best at that time, to feel, to see, to hear; at night one can be oneself. One can discard those innumerable masks one wears to face life. I had to do justice to Dru and her memory. I had go to her without a mask. She used to accuse me of confining myself to a role and projecting an image of a controlled man. The image has changed since then and at last I can feel with her in all her moments. She was controlled too, but even in those moments she caressed those she loved with her eyes. At that moment, sitting in Room 101 in the Palace Hotel at Maurya Nagar, it seemed as though no time had elapsed. Dru and I were sitting together, talking over a cup of tea. There was excitement in her face.

"I loved the book you gave me Vijay, *Psycho Cybernetics* by Maxwell Waltz. What have you observed?"

"You get influenced too easily. I am not you, Dru. I don't feel the same way. You see, each object has its own ability to absorb. Steel absorbs less than cloth and sponge absorbs a lot. I am like steel." She frowned.

"That's a strange analogy. The sponge may absorb a lot but you can squeeze it without effort. An ocean can absorb anything and yet retain its unique and indomitable character. And steel Vijay may not absorb anything but it melts when exposed to great heat."

"I can't help it, that's the way I am."

"You reject new ideas and their depth, their passion, nothing makes an impression on you. Let's finish the book Vijay, let there be an intellectual satisfaction in our relationship. There can be no other."

"I am an honest coward."

"Honest I am too, but not a coward. Most people circumvent their morality according to their needs. They conform because of social dictates, not necessarily because they believe in them. There are some of us who conform because of our beliefs and do not rationalise when it suits us. We emanate a moral force. It has become a rare concept."

"You are too confused."

I looked at the empty chair. There was no Dru. Memory was playing tricks on me. The agony of reminiscing was disturbed by the waiter who brought in the tea tray. The noise and clatter of cups and saucers drew my mind to the present. I was surprised to see two cups. Rather than correct the mistake made by room service, I poured tea into both and reverted to the cobwebs of the past.

"You are too earnest Dru. Whatever is moral for you may not be moral for another," I said, sipping my tea.

"The basic tenor of morality is universal Vijay, which one observes in dealing with human beings. We would be barbarians if each one of us decided to satisfy the animal urge which exists in all of us. The greatest crimes are committed in the name of religion and yet the essence of all religions is to love humanity."

"And what is your concept of humanity?" I asked, to humour her.

"My concept of humanity is a sincere involvement with the turbulence and rejoicing of another human being. We seem to have lost the capacity to give freely to those around us. Nor can we clearly define our relationship with the people with whom we share our lives."

The second cup was full, and mine was empty. Dru was a contradiction. Warm and gentle, she could become aloof in an instant. People mistook her gentleness for weakness. I couldn't hear her voice any more. I kept the cup on the table and thought of her with savage ferocity.

"I cannot endure pettiness and crudity," she used to say.

I was staring out of the window of the hotel, at Kismet. There was nothing to show that lively crowds must have once inhabited the place. It looked forlorn.

I turned around to get a better view of the room I was going to live in temporarily. It was a sprawling room. There was an olive green wall-to-wall carpet. On the left, stood a beautiful round table and two antique chairs made of wood with gold inlay. The double bed was placed in the middle. Two bedside lamps lit the room. The tapestry was deep blue and matched the bedspread. Blue raw-silk curtains covered the door. The crystal chandelier played musical notes. Close to the the window was a writing desk.

I entered an equally large bathroom fitted with marble tiles and a sunken bathtub. I saw my haggard face in the mirror and saw Dru (her hair was blowing in the breeze).

"Don't you see my face dancing on the pages of the book you are reading?"

"At the moment I am reading the Koran. All I see is Allah written there." Humour was my best defence.

She would never have compromised her world for me. Her objectives were very clear to her. She wanted me to acknowledge my love for her. My image of myself as a family man and a public servant was too powerful. She had never tresspassed into my domain, and I was afraid even of making a phone call to her.

"Why should you make me suffer because of your guilt?"

"Because you are the object of my guilt."

I did not visit her often because I feared that my wife Shanti would find out. I bound myself in a straitjacket. I am not proud of my behaviour any more.

"Why don't you tell her?"

"It is best not to get caught."

"I won't deceive anyone Vijay, not my husband, not my family, why should I deceive her as my friend? She will forgive you because she has to live with you. Why would she forgive me? I would have betrayed her as my friend. Love does not necessarily mean sex, love is also a communion of souls."

I came back to my room and sat down in the chair, staring at the cup of tea which looked as though someone had sipped it. She was incredible. It was not as though physical passions were dormant in her. She acknowledged them. I heard her voice again.

"I long for you Vijay. I long for your kisses, your caresses with an intensity which will surprise you. I masturbate when the gnawing need and the physical ache becomes unbearable. Night is my witness when I sob and cry in the darkness till sleep gathers me in its arms. But I won't allow it to happen. These are selfish needs which will satisfy us but hurt all those whom we love."

"Your husband doesn't seem to share your morality," I responded brutally.

"Oh Vijay! Your rationality perplexes me. Why should my values be affected by those around me? Yudhi didn't really love any other woman. They were conveniences in lonely moments. A temporary solace when I was not with him. No man or woman can come between Yudhi and I."

"But you did get hurt, Dru."

"Yes, I did get hurt. It set off a strange reaction in me. I too yearn for romance in my life. Someone who will find me beautiful. Someone who will love me. There were a few with whom I could have had an affair but I rejected them. My search came to an end when I met you. I remember that day: I felt like a sixteen year old girl who had discovered her first love. There was an inexplicable joy in my soul. I had rejuvenated the feminine mystique. If a husband could love another woman so could the wife love another man. My happiness was like an overflowing river. I waited for your phone calls; I waited for the sound of your car. One day when I was getting ready to meet you, my reflection in the mirror pointed a derisive finger at me. The room echoed with its jeering laughter."

"Dru, what a hypocrite you are," it said. "You judged Yudhi and now you are willing to compromise your values. Time is proving you wrong. A new love is exciting, romantic. Why shouldn't you give in? But how are you different, Dru? Where are your principles? I assume you will offer similar rationalisations. Where is your morality? Are you going to hurt Shanti?"

"No, no, no," I screamed and shut my ears, my eyes. Even my reflection seemed hideous to me and I wept at this vigilant flame within some of us which compels us to behave in a certain manner. "Yudhi may forgive me a discreet affair. But I will not hurt Shanti."

The vehemence of her reaction surprised me. I recalled Yudhi, Dru's husband. What had he done to deserve a woman like Dru? I had met Yudhi in Beirut and he had invited me to stay with him. He was a handsome fellow, six feet tall, very broad shouldered and weighed about two hundred odd pounds. He was heavy around his waist. He admitted he needed to lose weight but good food was his weakness. His neatly trimmed beard was greying. The hair on his shapely head was jet black. He had an enormous forehead, large laughing eyes, a straight nose and shapely lips. His chin was hidden by the beard. He could have been Adonis. I was awed by him. Yudhi was the most charming fellow in town and he knew it. He kept an open house. As the sun went down, people would start pouring in. It was a motley crowd that gathered there. Indian tourists who were short of foreign exchange were advised by travel agents to try his place. The atmosphere was that of an unending cocktail party. But at nine sharp he would pull down the shutters, except at weekends when there was no time limit. Yudhi said that there was no host in the house. That was rule number one. Other rules followed from this, such as help yourself and keep the kitchen clean: my wife hates a dirty kitchen. If someone wished to spend the night he had to inform Yudhi well in advance. And surprisingly enough, he would say no, not that night, some other night perhaps. That kept people guessing about what he wanted to do that night, but that also kept the club from becoming an inn. After nine in the evening Yudhi was a different man. I wondered whether he was the same person as the back-slapping, bear-hugging man we had met only a short while ago. He would change into normal clothes and go out for a drive or a drink at one of his favourite pubs and then end up for a good hearty meal in a restaurant. This excursion was always an exclusive affair. He picked his companions for this. They varied according to his mood. And they were never more than one or two, apart from me, that is. Every evening he selected a restaurant with care and deliberation. Sometimes it was a Chinese restaurant (only politics was discussed). Another day it was an Italian joint (painting and poetry were the subjects of discussion). An Indian restaurant was selected when the group discussed either sex or the miseries of the Indian under-dog. Dutch eating places were patronised when there was sea-food and good dancing and here, both on the menu and the topic of discussion, he didn't consult anyone. During my brief stay, he did me the courtesy of asking for my approval. When I left the choice to him he tried to match my selection to my mood.

"Vijay," he would say, "today you seem to be in the mood for a Chinese meal."

That gave me a great deal of amusement — that gesture, and his declaration that he was making it for my sake. I was touched. I admired his wit, though I was known as something of a humourist, but his humour was unique. Moreover, he could discuss Bach, Picasso, Indian classical music, politics , all with easy simplicity. Very few have this ability for we are inclined to boast, acquire a certain arrogance or become cynical. But Yudhi was sophisticated. I envied his zest for life. He introduced me to all the best life has to offer and brought me out of my conservative self. I thought that now I could discard my masks. But

I was wrong. It was difficult to break the iron chains of my inhibitions. On returning to my own environment I became the same, dull slogger. My greatest achievement was that of a humorist, for the mask of a humorist was indestructible. I enslaved my desires, my emotions in that image.

On the first two nights he allowed me to turn in early. The third evening he asked me if I liked to hit the pillow straight away or stay awake and gossip. He was a good conversationalist. I opted for gossip. It was around midnight. He poured himself a cognac and offered me one. I accepted. Dim lights lit the spacious living room. There was a family portrait on the table. He, his wife, a boy and two girls. The family portrait was informal -- another picture of his wife hung on the opposite wall, dominating the whole room.

The family portrait wasn't a studio one: everyone was dressed casually. They were sitting on a rock with the Mediterranean in the background. A picture of a happy family, one would say.

The picture on the wall was, however, different. There was something exclusive about her. She was smiling in a way that accentuated her dimples. The deep-set dark eyes spoke of a certain loneliness. She did not seem to be present in the picture.

"That's Dru, my wife. I took the picture myself after a bout of love making," he said with an impish grin.

That was my first introduction to Dru.

"Lovely family. And where are they now?"

"Oh, they are in India."

"You mean they don't live here?"

"No, not the children. They were with us for a while.

We thought they should be kept in residential schools where they could have an uninterrupted education, irrespective of our moving from place to place and Dru..." The symphony reached a crescendo. Yudhi's eyes became misty as they rested on Dru's photograph. He was not aware of me any more. Different feelings appeared on his handsome face, loneliness, tenderness and passion. She must be a remarkable person to arouse such feelings in a man like him, I thought to myself.

Yudhi looked at me.

"Dru is a utopian. We frail humans fall short of her standards. We painted a picture of a very sophisticated family, rich, cultured and all that bull-shit. Over the years she discovered how petty the god-damned powerful were; a joint-family in name where an individual's dignity was not recognised. She saw that the weak got abused. We failed her abjectly. She is too idealistic and I love her for her idealism. She kept a diary over the years. She wants to write a novel about us. The glory of our past and the ugliness of our present. 'Yudhi, I want a holiday from all of you. Give me a year, let me finish this book. I will become a hollow shell if I don't. You will not be happy living with a shadow,' she pleaded with me.

"In the past I had never stood in Dru's way. Everyone else mocked her. I had implicit faith in her ability. I had seen her grow from a naive girl to a mature lovely woman. I couldn't stop her. I long for her laughter which doesn't echo in the house anymore. I long for her lively conversation. You must have wondered why I don't allow anyone here after nine at night. Dru and I used to listen to music, or go out for a meal with a friend or two, not for idle chatter but serious conversation. 'I hate wastage of any kind Yudhi; intellectual or financial. Your family has wasted it all,' she would say.

"She will not come, nor will she call or write. Why don't you go and see her Vijay, she lives in your city, Chanakyapur. Perhaps you can help her with her manuscript."

I was deeply moved. I promised him that I would see her. It was almost dawn. The blue Mediterranean was tranquil. A few ripples played against Pigeon Rock. We went out onto the balcony and watched the sunrise.

"Dru used to give us scrambled eggs and toast here after our drinking bouts," he said, looking at the deep blue sea.

"Well, time we turn in; I have not been much company tonight."

"You were great." Instinctively I put my hand on his shoulder, a gesture I seldom indulge in.

Two days later I was back home and had to catch up with my pending files. On the third day I went to see Dru.

She received us -- my wife and I -- at the steps of her house and took us to the drawing room. The physical difference between Dru and Yudhi was staggering. She couldn't have been more than five feet two inches and weighed about a hundred and ten pounds. She had a round face, a very prominent straight nose, a large forehead, full lips and was dressed casually, in blue jeans and a blue shirt. She wore no make-up other than a light pink lipstick and black eyeliner. She was not the most beautiful woman I had seen, so why was she so different? I was dumbstruck! No witticisms, no humorous comments came forth that day. As a matter of fact I was the one who stammered.

Merriment flickered in her eyes.

The contours of her face lit up with an inscrutable smile. She had made another conquest.

She knew it.

What she did not reveal was that I had caused a stirring within her.

Sipping the coffee she had offered, I said, "Yudhi misses you. When are you going back?"

Her expression changed. Her eyes became serious. I couldn't read the depths of her anguish or loneliness.

"One day not too far from now, I will go back to him," she answered in a soft voice.

I didn't see her for about two weeks. She rang me up one morning.

"Vijay I want you to do me a favour. I can't trust anyone in this town."

"Well, I am honoured, what do you want me to do?"

"I need help. Will you read my manuscript and tell me whether I should go ahead with it?"

"Yes Dru, Yudhi told me about it. Let's meet at the club at seven. Bring the manuscript along."

We met the same evening. We did not have to wait long. Dru walked towards us wearing a brown printed maxi and a matching blouse. We sat in a secluded corner of the lawn in the club. Dru looked like a fragile plant caught in the tempest. She asked for rum. I was surprised at this choice of drink. Shanti and I ordered beer. It was a very pleasant evening. Dru had the capacity to make people feel at home. I had not felt such companionable serenity for a long time. She was a strange contrast to Shanti's constant demands. I could feel Shanti's indignation. It was clear that my association with Dru would lead to trouble. I did not care. I started to read the manuscript the next day. I couldn't put it down. It was a story of a girl growing into womanhood who is exposed to various influences, good and evil. She sets out on her own to formulate and prove her own value system. I was touched by the following passage in which Dru revealed her feelings for me along with a passionate urge to express herself in writing. The cynic in me doubted her authenticity while the writer in me was startled. Was she really genuine? Yes, I would like to help her. I would like to know Dru.

> "This inadequacy looms large and fierce like a guillotine perched over my head, ready to chop my neck, to dismember my head from my body. Why do I consort with these turbulent emotions? And this despair, this gnawing urge to communicate a vision?
>
> He is so near. The person who will understand, yet he is so remote. I can almost see him, hear him, feel the gentle throbbing of his heart and yet there is an insurmountable wall between us. Nature has not willed us to be lovers. I find myself impotent to grasp this opportunity. I can offer him my tender understanding. I can give myself totally to another in a different relationship.

> My love is a very powerful emotion. It has no frontiers. It has the capacity to absorb all relationships to the full. Perhaps I expect something after the love I bestow, but it's not for myself, it is for those around us. I give it without reservation because I love so completely. Again, I am lost in books today to smother my mounting desire to reach out to my love, to hear him, just to see him, to kill these fierce demons that have disturbed my equanimity. I have enslaved so many of my dreams. I will enslave this one too. My imagination will seek his comely face, his sensitive mind and perhaps his yearning too!

The intensity of her emotion enveloped me like a heavy mist. I was restless during the night, waiting for the morning when I could call her.

"Dru, I finished the manuscript last night."

The note of tenderness in my voice was like a flaming desire to protect her from everyone.

"What did you think of it, Vijay?"

She was hesitant, afraid of getting an adverse opinion.

"Not on the phone Dru, I will pick you up at eight. We are going to a friend's house for dinner, we'll talk there."

Dru was wearing a black sari. To my eyes she was the loveliest creature of God. The awareness of this new emotion made us both shy. Silently we savoured this wonderful feeling. She slid next to me in the car. I her held hand in mine. It was soft and warm. "How did you survive Dru?"

She smiled, "Oh, I managed."

The Manuscript

We picked up Shanti and went on to Moti's house. He was a loud-mouthed Punjabi who regaled his audience with dirty jokes. He was also a cynic who maintained that every man had a price. I don't know why I ever chose him as a friend.

The room was lit with chandeliers. There was a beautiful painting of a Banjara woman in orange oil colour on the wall. There was music on the hi-fi. I took Dru to the dance floor and held her close to me. She moved gracefully to the music. We didn't talk. I caressed her cheek with my lips. She was startled. She looked into my eyes with grave intensity and whispered, "I have never felt like this for anyone except Yudhi."

Dru left the next day for Maurya Nagar. By a strange coincidence of fate two people had fallen in love. I missed her. Her absence had left a void in my life. This was the beginning of our relationship. My knowledge of her was directly from her manuscript. Years proved that Dru was no masquerador of her feelings. Her world understood our relationship. I couldn't explain it to mine.

I looked out. The hotel clock chimed and the hands of my watch showed that the time was ten o'clock. The food on the tray had gone cold. I poured myself a cup of tea and continued my reverie. Dru came back next week. I used to go to see her at her house. She was invariably working on the manuscript.

"Keep your papers away Dru," I'd gather her in my arms and kiss her.

"Vijay, Vijay, we are supposed to work on the manuscript," she'd remind me gently, freeing herself from my embrace.

"There is always a tomorrow. Let's go for a drive."

The car sped on the straight unending road, as though destined for the horizon, away from the curious eyes of society. I felt free and bouyant. I stopped near a field. She rolled up her trousers, left her high heels in the car. I walked with her hand in mine through the puddles and the soft grass till we reached a shady spot under the rock. We sat against the rough surface, uncomfortable yet oblivious of everything except each other. I kissed her soft lips. My desire to make love to her was obvious.

She placed her finger on my lips: "Hush Vijay, no. I am an unusual woman. Can't we love each other without having an affair?"

The memory of Dru is like a wound which time has not healed. Her moments of gaiety and pain are two faces I am unable to forget. She was a regular visitor to the house. My children became very fond of her. After the initial hostility Shanti changed her opinion of Dru and accepted her as a friend. We became a threesome. It was Dru now who had reason to fret. Shanti did not permit me to finish the manuscript with Dru. I bought peace again. I compromised. Shanti had her way as usual. Dru's manuscript didn't get a chance. What Shanti couldn't do was to draw me away from Dru. I loved her and wanted her. I believed that if pursued she would give in.

"I want to make love to you Dru."

"One night of lovemaking cannot affect years of loneliness. And what's more, you have used Shanti to be a friend of mine."

Men seldom accept defeat in pursuit of a woman.

It was harder for me, for I loved Dru, and couldn't accept that she wouldn't give in. It was a hot summer afternoon. The sun was blazing outside. Because of a power cut the air-conditioner was not working. I could feel intense heat crawling down my spine and attacking my groin. I picked up the phone and dialled her number.

"Dru did I wake you?"

"The fact that you called, Vijay, compensates for the loss of sleep."

"Are you free this evening?"

"Even if I was busy, I'd cancel the appointment to be with you."

"Dru, come to Moti's house at 9 o'clock tonight. Don't forget," I added, breathless with emotion.

"I won't forget."

She was there at the appointed hour. I was delayed. Moti received her. She felt awkward and restless. She sat in a corner of the sofa smoking a cigarette. Moti was in a flurry. He got up and paced the room, picking up a glass, playing a record.

"Would you like a drink?"

"Yes please. Rum and soda with a little ice."

Moti gave her the drink and sat down.

"Is it O.K?"

"Yes thank you. I wonder why Vijay and Shanti are so late. Perhaps I should call them."

"Oh no, don't do that," he said, flinging his arms about and gesticulating with great vehemence.

"I called them some time ago. They are not at home," he added. "You have written a novel I believe."

"I am trying to write one. I hear a car. I think the Mehtas have come."

I walked in alone. She was surprised. She had no idea of the setup.

"How is it that you are alone?"

"I had to go to an official function."

I sat next to her, lit one of her cigarettes and inhaled deeply. The ambience was the same, so was Dru. I wanted her passionately. I took her to the verandah and kissed her.

"Oh Vijay, an hour in the evening doesn't resolve a relationship. You have to work out a solution on a day-to-day basis."

"I love you Dru. I want to make love to you."

"No Vijay, No." She smelt of rum and cigarettes. My lips caressed her lips, her face, her eyes, her neck. I loved her. No other woman had aroused this passionate physical longing in me. I wanted her in bed. I thought at last our love will be consummated. We danced, oblivious of Moti and his girlfriend. That evening I wasn't masquerading. I was plain Vijay Mehta who loved this wispy woman in his arms.

"I am the only woman you have ever loved Vijay."

"Yes, yes."

I buried my head on her shoulder, hugging her closer. The music ended. She excused herself to go to the toilet. A few minutes later I followed her to the adjoining bedroom.

"I knew you'd come here Vijay. I am not the type who gives in. I really mean what I say. . ."

I didn't let her finish the sentence. I kissed her again and made her lie down on the bed. My hand was caressing her soft thigh.

"Go away Vijay, leave me alone. You look like any lecherous man. I thought you were different. We have an intellectual commitment to each other. I love you very much but I must not fail. Leave me alone."

I could hear the pounding of her heart. She pushed me away without a qualm, opened the door and went out without a backward glance.

I felt indignant, humiliated and furious. No woman had brushed me off so ruthlessly. There were many who would have happily had an affair with me. I had rejected them. It was I who wanted to love a woman with principles and, to my consternation, had discovered Dru. . . Dru who confessed her deep love but would not compromise her morality. I brushed my hair and waited for a while to compose myself.

Dru was talking to Moti and his girlfriend. She was calm and continued her conversation without guile or embarrassment. I sat next to her feeling gauche. I felt as though I had behaved like a villain.

"Come on. I will drop you home."

"Let me finish my drink. What's the rush? It's not often that I see you alone."

She appraised me frankly and took her time finishing her drink. I was trying to control the rage within me. She said goodbye to Moti without batting an eyelid and sat in the car.

"Bye Moti, thanks for everything."

"I am sorry things didn't. . ."

"Forget it."

I was unusually quiet. So was she. It seemed as though she had dismissed the events of the evening for there were no accusations hurled at me. It was natural for me to want her and I suppose it was her right to reject my advances. She was sitting close to the door.

"Just drive on Vijay. Don't drop me home. I want to savour this moment."

"No, it's late. I have to be home."

"Vijay, say something. Talk about anything."

I am not a man of many words and am basically a shy person. I was reflecting on the events of the evening. I was annoyed, overwhelmed, awed. I loved her.

We reached her home. I kissed her. She did not respond.

"Good night, Dru. See you sometime."

"When will that be?"

"I don't know."

I realised my limbs were aching. I got up from the chair and looked out of the window. It was ten thirty. Outside, everything was still. Nothing stirred except the ghosts in my memory. My thoughts rambled on.

From that night our relationship changed. Dru wasn't a starry-eyed romantic fool like most women. I had to deal with her mind. I couldn't have hurt her more: yes, she was deeply hurt. She stopped asking me to help her with the manuscript. She wanted me to acknowledge an intellectual equality between us. I had behaved like a self-centred and self-involved pompous fool. She had a terrible habit of smoking a cigarette before going to sleep. That night her bed caught fire. She woke up screaming. The room was full of smoke. Her feet and legs were burnt.

"It was a bad omen, a warning from the gods," she remarked.

I couldn't understand her. She bewildered me.

"Dru, you are superstitious."

"Yes."

"You smoke and you drink and you are acquiring a terrible reputation. Go to an ashram and purify yourself."

"You are judging me for smoking and drinking. You should be ashamed of yourself."

"Why should I be ashamed of myself? Everyone is talking about it—your friends I mean."

"I don't care about them. I only cry about what you think."

"If you are not bothered. . ."

"No, I am not. I am glad to be different. I am not a shadow of my husband for I have a distinct personality of my own. Neither do I whine and make his life a misery for I have the ability to amuse myself. Others pick on me for self authentication."

"You are mad."

"You seem to have an irresistible affinity to mad people. I assume Shanti and women like her seem moral and traditional to you."

"Yes."

"It is easy to play a traditional role enclosed within the four walls of a room. But to remain pure, when you are a part of the world, meeting different kinds of people, requires a certain kind of character which they do not have. I am surprised that you don't see through this flimsy facade."

Sometimes I moved into a world of fantasy, a new

city, a different environment where we could be together, unknown, in an alien place.

"You seem to have a convenient morality. A change of scene and you are ready to shed your inhibitions! I believe in not hurting another human being. You only see my weaknessess, smoking and drinking and not my strengths. To me the concept of a friend is more important than the consummation of love."

I was impressed and ashamed that I had criticised her for her drinking and smoking.

She responded with cold hauteur.

"I smoke to burn the phallic symbols around me with a match box. And what's more, you make me sound like an alcoholic. I'm not. I keep good company these days."

"You have improved," I agreed.

"Your gift to me is stability. The control of the establishment, but your establishment can be stifling. It is full of mediocrity. It forces people to follow a prescribed pattern. It subtly tyrannises people who are different. I find it amazing that you take your profession so seriously and yet in your daily lives you compromise, you overlook injustices. You live in your cocoon and ignore everything else, poverty, ugliness, hunger, emaciated bodies. Nothing seems to touch you. You allow the establishment to take over. My quarrel is with you and only you. You live a dual role."

Suddenly, the room was in darkness. Power shortage again, I gathered. A few minutes later, the lights came on.

I could not efface my upbringing. Neither could I negate beliefs instilled in me; nor could I tell my friends and family that I had lived a dual role. I had tried to believe in my work. The only thing that kept me sane was writing. Even my writing was subject to the social order; none of my desires, dreams and aspirations sought my pen. No social upheavals took place because of my ideas. My wife was always the heroine. I described her as a fair woman who loved me. I was grateful. My public image of a family man remained spotless. I thrived. Dru came along and caused ripples. Ripples are not formed in steel. I was an intellectual coward for I was unable to break the iron chains of the establishment. Dru's enemy was her idealism. Or so I thought. She went away from my life, leaving the following note for me.

> A few encounters in a brief sojourn fade out and become memories in the recesses of the mind. A few are sensual, momentary, for the satiation of sexual need. A few are like beacons and yet admonished, repulsed. I wonder what happens to those concords? Do they fade away? Or are they like a flame, attempting to enlighten the world? It would be a pity if these were buried in dust. It would be sacrilegious to flick them away like annoying bees. He was undermining the innocence of the relationship. She suffered indignity although she contributed laughter and gaiety in his life. Will the absence of her calm disposition cause anguish in him? Ah! where are those loves and lovers for whom Taj Mahal was built? *Adieu.*

"Going for a breath of fresh air, sir?"
"Yes, I think I will take a look at Kismet."
"The old retainer is usually awake at this time."

I left my key at the desk and walked out into the calm night. It was a very pleasant walk. Kismet was only a furlong away. The gate was closed. I stood there for a few minutes and called out.

"*Koi hai* (is someone there)?"

"Hello Satan," I managed to say, and stroked his black coat.

"You know, Vijay, Satan is almost human," Dru had said. He was lonely and he knew I was a friend.

The old man had reached the gate now. He was wearing white trousers and a white shirt. There was a towel tied around his head. He must be Muthu.

"No one lives here sahib."

"Muthu, I came to see the place. I used to know Dru amma."

"Come in Sahib. Dru amma left this place many years ago."

"Yes, I know."

"I am planting trees to give us roots."

The trees had weathered the storms. Four steps and we were on the verandah which was covered with a wooden structure.

There was a glass door leading to the drawing room. Muthu had reverently covered everything with dust sheets. On the left was a swing.

"Do you want to see Dru amma's bedroom?"

"Yes."

I drew a deep breath. Muthu took me through the garden again. There was a circular glass window on the left. We had come to the front of the house. He opened the door. Each nerve in my body was throbbing. Dru looked different. She smiled. She wasn't alone any more. I had come to her at last. There was only a divan against the wall, a writing desk, a chair and a painting of a parrot in a cage. A brass standard lamp was lying nearby.

"Light the lamp Muthu and wait for me outside."

I felt a gradual awakening of my senses as I walked towards her desk. The first thing I noticed was Yudhi's photograph in his A.D.C's uniform. A few of my books were neatly stacked against a bookstand; anguish spread like a heat wave making me perspire in that tranquil and cool night. I saw my letters. I threw them away in the waste paper basket. I had never really discerned Dru's emotional nature. Suddenly, I felt enveloped in the warmth of her love. My superficial veneer fell away. I opened the drawer of the desk and found the manuscript. Composing myself, I came out of the room.

"Have you found your papers, sahib?"

"How do you know I was looking for papers, Muthu?"

"Dru amma said you will come for them one day."

The Remains of the Feast

GITHA HARIHARAN

THE ROOM STILL smells of her. Not as she did when she was dying, an overripe smell that clung to everything that had touched her, sheets, saris, hands. She had been in the nursing home for only ten days but a bedsore grew like an angry red welt on her back. Her neck was a big hump, and she lay in bed like a moody camel that would snap or bite at unpredictable intervals. The goitred lump, the familiar swelling I had seen on her neck all my life, that I had stroked and teasingly pinched as a child, was now a cancer that spread like a fire down the old body, licking clean everything in its way.

The room now smells like a pressed, faded rose. A dry, elusive smell. Burnt, a candle put out.

We were not exactly roommates, but we shared two rooms, one corner of the old ancestral house, all my twenty-year old life.

She was Rukmini, my great-grandmother. She was ninety when she died last month, outliving by ten years her only son and daughter-in-law. I don't know how she felt then, but later she seemed to find something slightly hilarious about it all. That she, an ignorant village-bred woman, who signed the papers my father brought her with a thumb print, should survive; while they, city-bred, ambitious, should collapse of weak hearts and arthritic knees at the first sign of old age.

Her sense of humour was always quaint. It could also be embarrassing. She would sit in her corner, her round plump face reddening, giggling like a little girl. I knew better than ask her why, I was a teenager by then. But some uninitiated friend would be unable to resist, and would go up to my great-grandmother and ask her why she was laughing. This, I knew, would send her into uncontrollable peals. The tears would flow down her cheeks, and finally, catching her breath, still weak with laughter, she would confess. She could fart exactly like a train whistling its way out of the station, and it gave her as much joy as a child would get when she saw, or heard, a train.

So perhaps it is not all that surprising that she could be flippant about her only child's death, especially since ten years had passed.

"Yes, Ratna, you study hard and become a big doctor, madam," she would chuckle when I kept the lights on all night and paced up and down the room, reading to myself.

"The last time I saw a doctor, I was thirty years old. Your grandfather was in the hospital for three months. He would faint every time he saw his own blood."

And, as if that summed up the progress made between two generations, she would pull her blanket over her head and begin snoring almost immediately.

I have two rooms, the entire downstairs, to myself now since my great-grandmother died. I begin my course at medical college next month, and I am afraid to be here alone at night.

I have to live up to the gold medal I won last year. I keep late hours, reading my anatomy textbook before the course begins. The body is a solid, reliable thing. It is a wonderful, resilient machine. I hold on to the thick, hardbound book and flip through the new smelling pages greedily. I stop every time I find an illustration and look at it closely. It reduces us to pink, blue and white colour-coded, labelled parts. Muscles, veins, tendons. Everything has a name. Everything is linked, one with the other, all parts of a functioning whole.

It is poor consolation for the nights I have spent in her warm bed, surrounded by that safe, familiar, musty smell.

She was cheerful and never sick. But she was also undeniably old, and so it was no great surprise to us when she suddenly took to lying in bed all day a few weeks before her ninetieth birthday.

She had been lying in bed for close to two months, ignoring concern, advice, scolding, and then she suddenly gave up. She agreed to see a doctor.

The young doctor came out of her room, his face puzzled and angry. My father begged him to sit down and drink a cup of hot coffee.

"She will need all kinds of tests," he announced. "How long has she had that lump on her neck? Have you had it checked?"

My father shifted uneasily in his cane chair. He is a cadaverous looking man, prone to nervousness and sweating. He keeps a big jar of antacids on his office desk. He has a nine to five accountant's job in a government owned company, the kind that never fires its employees.

My father pulled out the small towel he uses in place of a handkerchief. Wiping his forehead, he mumbled, "You know how these old women are. Impossible to argue with them."

"The neck," the doctor said, more gently. I could see he pitied my father.

"I think it was examined once, long ago. My father was alive then. There was supposed to have been an operation, I think. But you know what they thought in those days. An operation meant an unnatural death. All the relatives came over to scare her, advise her with horror stories. So she said no. You know how it is. And she was already a widow then, my father was the head of the household. How could he, a fourteen-year old, take the responsibility?"

"Well," said the doctor. He shrugged his shoulders. "Let me know when you want to admit her in my nursing home. But I suppose it's best to let her die at home."

When the doctor left, we looked at each other, the three of us, like shifty accomplices. My mother, practical as always, broke the silence and said, "Let's not tell her anything. Why worry her? And then we'll have all kinds of difficult old aunts and cousins visiting, it will be such a nuisance. How will Ratna study in the middle of all that chaos?"

But when I went to our room that night, my great-grandmother had a sly look on her face. "Come here, Ratna," she said. "Come here, my darling little gem."

I went, my heart quaking at the thought of telling her.

She held my hand and kissed each finger, her half-closed eyes almost flirtatious. "Tell me something, Ratna," she began in a wheedling voice.

"I don't know, I don't know anything about it," I said quickly.

"Of course you do." She was surprised, a little annoyed. "Those small cakes you got from the Christian shop that day. Do they have eggs in them?"

"Do they?" she persisted. "Will you," and her eyes narrowed with cunning, "will you get one for me?"

So we began a strange partnership, my great-grandmother and I. I smuggled cakes and ice cream, biscuits and samosas, made by non-Brahmin hands, into a vegetarian invalid's room. To the deathbed of a Brahmin widow who had never eaten anything but pure, home-cooked food for almost a century.

She would grab it from my hand, late at night after my parents had gone to sleep. She would hold the pastry in her fingers, turn it round and round, as if on the verge of an earthshaking discovery.

"And does it really have an egg in it?", she would ask again, as if she needed the password for her to bite into it with her gums.

"Yes, yes," I would say, a little tired of midnight feasts by then. The pastries were a cheap yellow colour, topped by white frosting with hard grey pearls.

The Remains of the Feast 141

"Lots and lots of eggs," I would say, wanting her to hurry up and put it in her mouth. "And the bakery is owned by a Christian. I think he hires Muslim cooks too."

"Ooooh," she would moan. Her little pink tongue darted out and licked the frosting. Her toothless mouth worked its way steadily, munching, making happy sucking noises.

Our secret was safe for about a week. Then she become bold. She was bored with the cakes, she said. They gave her heartburn. She became a little more adventurous every day. Her cravings were various and unpredictable. Laughable and always urgent.

"I'm thirsty," she moaned, when my mother asked her if she wanted anything. "No, no, I don't want water, I don't want juice." She stopped the moaning and looked at my mother's patient, exasperated face. "I'll tell you what I want," she whined. "Get me a glass of that brown drink Ratna bought in the bottle. The kind that bubbles and makes a popping sound when you open the bottle. The one with the fizzy noise when you pour it out."

"A coca-cola?" said my mother, shocked. "Don't be silly, it will make you sick."

"I don't care what it is called," my great-grandmother said and started moaning again. "I want it."

So she got it and my mother poured out a small glassful, tight-lipped, and gave it to her without a word. She was always a dutiful grand-daughter-in-law.

"Ah," sighed my great-grandmother, propped up against her pillows, the steel tumbler lifted high over her lips. The lump on her neck moved in little gurgles as she drank. Then she burped a loud, contented burp and asked, as if she had just thought of it, "Do you think there is something in it? You know, alcohol?"

A month later, we had got used to her new, unexpected, inappropriate demands. She had tasted, by now, lemon tarts, garlic, three types of aereated drinks, fruit cake laced with brandy, bhel-puri from the fly-infested bazaar nearby.

"There's going to be trouble," my mother kept muttering under her breath. "She's losing her mind, she is going to be a lot of trouble."

And she was right, of course. My great-grandmother could no longer swallow very well. She would pour the coke into her mouth and half of it would trickle out of her nostrils, thick, brown, nauseating.

"It burns, it burns," she would yell then, but she pursed her lips tightly together when my mother spooned a thin gruel into her mouth. "No, no," she screamed deliriously. "Get me something from the bazaar. Raw onions. Fried bread. Chickens and goats."

Then we knew she was lost to us. She was dying.

She was in the nursing home for ten whole days. My mother and I took turns sitting by her, sleeping on the floor by the hospital cot.

She lay there quietly, the pendulous neck almost as big as her face. But she would not let the nurses near her bed. She would squirm and wriggle like a big fish that refused to be caught. The sheets smelled, and the young doctor shook his head. "Not much to be done now," he said. "The cancer has left nothing intact."

The day she died, she kept searching the room with

her eyes. Her arms were held down by the tubes and needles, criss-cross, in, out. The glucose dripped into her veins but her nose still ran, the clear, thin liquid trickling down like dribble onto her chin. Her hands clenched and unclenched with the effort and she whispered, like a miracle, "Ratna."

My mother and I rushed to her bedside. Tears streaming down her face, my mother bent her head before her and pleaded, "Give me your blessings, Pati. Bless me before you go."

My great-grandmother looked at her for a minute, her lips working furiously, noiselessly. For the first time in my life I saw a fine veil of perspiration on her face. The muscles on her face twitched in mad, frenzied jerks. Then she pulled one arm free of the tubes, in a sudden, crazy spurt of strength, and the I.V. pole crashed to the floor.

"Bring me a red sari," she screamed. "A red one with a big wide border of gold. And," her voice cracked, "bring me peanuts with chili powder from the corner shop. Onion and green chili bondas deep fried in oil."

Then the voice gurgled and gurgled, her face and neck swayed, rocked like a boat lost in a stormy sea. She retched, and as the vomit flew out of her mouth, her nose, thick like the milkshakes she had drunk, brown like the alcoholic coke, her head slumped forward, her rounded chin buried in the cancerous neck.

When we brought the body home — I am not yet a doctor and already I can call her that — I helped my mother to wipe her clean with a wet, soft cloth. We wiped away the smells, the smell of the hospital bed, the smell of an old woman's juices drying. Her skin was dry and papery. The stubble on her head — she had refused to shave her head once she got sick — had grown, like the soft, white bristles of a hairbrush.

She had had only one child though she had lived so long. But the skin on her stomach was like crumpled, frayed velvet, the creases running to and fro in fine, silvery rivulets.

"Bring her sari," my mother whispered, as if my great-grandmother could still hear her.

I looked at the stiff, cold body that I was seeing naked for the first time. She was asleep at last, quiet at last. I had learnt, in the last month or two, to expect the unexpected from her. I waited, in case she changed her mind and sat up, remembering one more taboo food to be tasted.

"Bring me your eyebrow tweezers," I heard her say. "Bring me that hair-removing cream. I have a moustache and I don't want to be an ugly old woman."

But she lay still, the wads of cotton in her nostrils and ears shutting us out. Shutting out her belated ardour.

I ran to my cupboard and brought her the brightest, reddest sari I could find: last year's Divali sari, my first silk. I unfolded it, ignoring my mother's eyes which were turning aghast. I covered her naked body lovingly. The red silk glittered like her childish laughter.

"Have you gone mad?" my mother whispered furiously. "She was a sick old woman, she didn't know what she was saying." She rolled up the sari and flung it aside, as if it had been polluted. She wiped the body again to free it from foolish, trivial desires.

They burnt her in a pale brown sari, her widow's weeds. The prayer beads I had never seen her touch encircled the bulging, obscene neck.

I am still a novice at anatomy. I hover just over the body, I am just beneath the skin. I have yet to look at the insides, the entrails of memories she told me nothing about, the pain congealing into a cancer.

She has left me behind with nothing but a smell, a legacy that grows fainter every day. I haunt the dirtiest bakeries and tea-stalls I can find every evening. I search for her, my sweet great-grandmother, in plate after plate of stale confections, in needle sharp green chilies deep-fried in rancid oil. I plot her revenge for her, I give myself diarrhoea for a week.

Then I open all the windows and her cupboard and air the rooms. I tear her dirty grey saris to shreds. I line the shelves of her empty cupboard with my thick, newly-bought, glossy-jacketed texts, one next to the other. They stand straight and solid, row after row of armed soldiers. They fill up the small cupboard in minutes.

Mallika Farida

SHALINI SARAN

WHEN FARIDA WAS a child, her grandmother, Ammijan, told her a story every afternoon. Ammijan's stories were about kings and wise men, and magical serpents that had jewels hidden in the dark recesses of their throats. But Farida's favourite story was about the earthquake which took place at the time of her birth.

"Tell me, Ammijan," she would say, "tell me what happened when I was born."

Ammijan would conceal a smile, put aside her sewing, and ask, "Again?"

And Farida would nod her head firmly and say, "Yes. Again."

So the old woman would begin anew, about that night when, fresh from the womb, Farida lay beside her mother. On that dark, moonless night the dogs had started to bark and the birds had become restless. Then a deep, rumbling sound had arisen as the earth trembled violently. The villagers had run out of their houses, screaming with terror, but Farida's mother was too weak to move. So the little family had huddled over its firstborn, praying to Allah for mercy. And Allah, who is full of compassion, had protected them from the wrath of nature.

When Farida first heard this story she had asked, "What is compassion?"

And Ammijan had answered, "When you look on the world with love in your heart, that is compassion. Allah is the Compassionate One."

"Why, then, Ammijan," the little girl had exclaimed, "Allah must be just like you. For *you* look on *everyone* with love in your heart."

"Oh. . . hush child. . .", the old woman had said in a shocked whisper. "Be off with you!"

Farida had sauntered off, smiling with satisfaction, her heart warmed by the thought of Allah being just like her Ammijan.

Forty years later Farida found her way to the medieval shrine where the Sufi saint, known as the Protector of the Poor, lay buried. The shrine was in the heart of the city, and clinging to its periphery was a slum — home to ragpickers and rickshaw-pullers, criminals and drug-addicts, vermin and vice. Farida, like many others, had come here in search of shelter.

For the first few days Farida lingered in the courtyard of the mausoleum, keenly observing her new surroundings. At night she retired to the pilgrim's serai. When she decided to make inquiries about a room for herself, she was directed to Mirza Sahib, a keeper of the shrine. He, in fact, had noticed her soon after her arrival. One could not but do so.

Farida was graceful and composed; her gaze was clear and steady. In a crowd, she stood apart.

Mirza Sahib sat beside the donation box, near the doorway to the saint's tomb. When Farida approached him with her request he looked at her coldly, and asked, "Where have you come from?"

"From Basera. . ."

"Where is that?"

"It is a village. . . near Mandu. . ."

"And your family?"

"I have no family. . ."

Mirza Sahib led her down an alley which skirted the stepped well. The "room" he showed her comprised of the graves of two long-forgotten noblemen. A marble canopy resting on four ornate pillars served as a roof over this space which Mirza Sahib had enclosed with planks of wood.

"I have even made a window," he said, "and a door which can be locked. So I will charge you thirty rupees a month. . ."

Farida accepted the offer.

"How will you earn a living?" Mirza Sahib asked, suspiciously.

"With my two hands," Farida answered.

Mirza Sahib was taken aback by her forthright answer. "Be sure to bring the money immediately," he said, as he walked back to the shrine. "You'll have to pay on the first of every month, or else. . . And yes," he paused to add, "remember, this is sacred ground. If you can't live like a decent woman, it's better you find a place in the slum."

Farida gathered her meagre belongings and went to Mirza Sahib who was back at his usual place.

"Here is the money," she said.

Mirza Sahib thrust the notes into his pocket. He felt uneasy; he felt as though Farida's eyes looked through him. He felt the need to reaffirm his spiritual status.

"Do you read the Koran?" he asked her.

"I don't read," Farida answered.

"Do you pray five times a day?"

Farida remained silent.

"What kind of woman are you?" he asked, his eyes narrowing. "Do you know anything about your religion?"

Farida looked at him with her clear, still eyes, and said, "I know that Allah is compassionate."

And again, Mirza Sahib was taken aback.

Farida examined her strange dwelling closely, wondering about the men who lay buried there. The room was about seven feet long and nine feet wide, and the brick floor was pitted and uneven. The partially damaged graves defined spaces which, she noted, could be used for cooking, storing and sewing —— a skill which she had learnt from her Ammijan. Only the marble roof and the ornate pillars were smooth and unbroken, and seemed, therefore, all the more incongruous. The window overlooked the green waters of the stepped well far down below. The door opened into the alley which led to the shrine on one side, and the slum on the other. The "room" lay poised in between. Farida could hear the qawwals at the shrine; she was close enough to the slum to be aware of its lingering stench.

She had barely set down her belongings when word spread in the slum that old Mirza Sahib's "palace" had been given to a woman. The news gave rise to curiosity and lewd conjecture. Who was this woman? What was she doing here? Was she like one of them? Kalua, who also owned the tea stall, wondered if she would join his gang of ragpickers. Khema, the notorious pimp, savoured the prospect of another commodity he could sell.

"Oh. . . I wouldn't be so sure," said Kalua. "They say she looks different. Besides," he added, referring to the graves, "she'll be sleeping with two princes. . ." Raucous laughter followed Kalua's remarks.

In a few days, everyone knew of her name and of her intention to earn a living by sewing. But an air of mystery hung about Farida, for she revealed nothing of herself. When asked about her life, she would smile her enigmatic smile, and say, "I am just a traveller passing through. . ."

Farida was fortunate to find work with Salim — "Master Salim" as the tailor was known. His shop was nearby, in the marketplace, and he was, like all ladies' tailors, overworked and prone to fluctuating moods. He gave Farida those garments which needed to be hand-stitched — she looked clean and reliable — and he also gave her sequins to tack on to yards of silk and georgette. Master Salim knew Mirza Sahib, he knew where his "palace" was. Farida could take the cloth home, he said. And he would pay her according to the work she did. The arrangement suited Farida. When she walked out of the shop with her bundle of silk and sequins, she felt at peace.

Farida kept away from the slum; she rarely visited the shrine. Her life acquired a steady rhythm. She would start sewing in the morning after completing her chores, and work through the day till there was light enough. While she worked, she kept her door ajar. Farida, seated between the graves, with swirls of silk and heaps of glittering sequins about her, became a familiar sight to passers-by. Women and children from the slum would often pause to speak with her. She looked like a queen, they said, a queen on a throne of marble. And they started to call her Mallika Farida. The men, too, were secretly in awe of her. Even Khema hesitated to approach her, though he often boasted that one day he would make her the queen of the slum.

As the days went by the women began to tell Farida about their lives, for at her doorstep they found a hitherto unknown calm. Farida would sew her sequins while they talked. She listened silently to sordid details of the violence and the indignity which seemed a part of survival in the slum. Farida was not always sympathetic; at times the women were provoked by her responses. But they drew courage from her –– Rashida, Shanno Chukki –– they all unburdened themselves and found comfort in their Mallika Farida.

For a while nothing altered the scheme of Farida's life. On the first of every month she paid her rent to Mirza Sahib, though rarely was a word exchanged between them. Farida earned enough to feed herself. More and more women confided in her, and found solace in her. There were brawls and bickerings as usual in the slum. On Thursday evenings the crowds grew at the shrine, and the qawwals sang late into the night. After the blistering heat of summer came the soothing monsoon.

One day, Chukki asked Farida, "Will you teach us to sew as finely as you do?"
 Farida smiled, and said, "Of course."
 "You see, then we may not be at Khema's mercy..."
 "You are right."
 The next afternoon five women came to Farida. "Please, please do close the door," they said. "We do not want our menfolk to know... as yet..."
 Farida gave them some discarded rags, and needle and thread, and she taught them to sew just as Ammijan had once taught her. But in the slum nothing could remain a secret for long. A week later, as Chukki was returning from her sewing lesson, Khema obstructed her path. His eyes were bloodshot, and he reeked of alcohol.
 "You stay away from that queen of yours, do you understand?" he said in an ugly, menacing voice.
 The next day, when Farida remarked upon Chukki's absence, the women looked at one another.
 "Khema has threatened her," said Rashida.
 "And if he threatens you, will you, too, cease to come?" The women remained silent.
 Khema did threaten them. But they came -- the next day, the day after and again, the day after. So Khema changed his ploy. That afternoon, when he saw the

women going to Farida's room, he shouted, "I will prove to you that your queen is a whore. . . just like the rest of you. Tell her that I will visit her tonight. As for that bolt on the door. . . tell her it can't keep Khema away. . ."

The women feared for their Mallika Farida who provided them a haven and gave them hope. When they conveyed the news to her in terrified whispers, she turned pale, but said, "Let him come. . ."

And each woman wondered to herself, is Khema right after all?

That evening Farida did not close her door as usual after sunset. And Khema -- who had grown from foundling to street urchin to petty thief and was now barely human -- Khema entered her room and bolted the door behind him.

In the slum, the menfolk jeered at their women: "Know where Khema's gone tonight?. . . to your queen. . . with her silks and fancy ideas. . . that's where Khema has gone. Now she will indeed become the queen of the slum. . ."

And the women were mortified into silence.

The next morning there was an air of anticipation at Kalua's tea stall. It was time for Khema to come. He would have something new to tell them, some bawdy tale perhaps about the old prude. . . But when Khema appeared for his usual cup of tea, he was silent. The men asked:

"Had a good time?"

"What was she like?"

"Did you bring her to life between the dead?"

To their surprise, Khema only said, "Leave me

alone."

"What? Fallen in love, have you?"

"Would you believe it," said Kalua in exaggerated tones, "our Khema, king of the slum. . . terror of the underworld. . . demon of the night. . . our Khema has fallen in love!"

Khema flung his empty teacup on the table. "Shut up, you swine," he growled, and walked away.

"What's got into *him*?" Kalua muttered, retrieving the bits of broken china.

The women talked amongst themselves, torn between disappointment and the hope that perhaps all this was not true. They went to Farida, as usual, in the afternoon. Face to face with her, they could only mumble in bewildered voices:

"You, of all people. . ."

"How could you. ."

"Did he really. ."

"Why did you. ."

Farida, who looked drawn and distant, said quietly, "Only Allah will understand why. . ." Then she proceeded with the lesson.

Khema did not emerge from his hovel the whole day. He refused to speak with anyone. But in the evening, Amar, his childhood friend and accomplice prevailed upon him. "What's the matter with you?" he shouted, exasperated. "What has she done to you? What was she like. . . ?"

And Khema whispered, ". . . like. . . like the home . . . the oasis. . . the stable earth. . ."

A few days later Farida went to pay her rent. Mirza Sahib looked more severe than ever. "I've been hearing things about you," he said accusingly.

"Such as. . . ?"

"Such as Khema. . . of all the notorious men. . . Khema. . . huh. I'm warning you; I'm giving you one more chance. Remember what I told you when I gave you protection. If you can't live like a decent woman then look for shelter in that filthy slum. Remember," he added coldly, "you are living on sacred ground . . . this is a sacred shrine. . ."

Farida looked at him steadily. "Mirza Sahib," she said, "there is no shrine as sacred as one's body. . ."

The Tamarind Tree Murder

URMILA BANERJEE

THEY'D FOUND THE body in a locked room. With barred windows and the fan in motion.

Her name was Ratnabali Lahiri -- she had been as elegant as her name and she was sixty-five when she died.

I remember that room well -- the way the sunlight would play on one wall, like waves. And beyond the bars, banana trees in the garden, their fronds green in the Calcutta sun.

The newspaper report said that she had been a great beauty once -- Ratnabali Lahiri, wife of the late Justice Lahiri. A pillow with a delicate floral cover had been found on the floor beside her bed -- the murder weapon.

There were bruises on her face, signs of resistance, and then, I suppose, she went limp.

"But if the door was locked," my mother later said, "how did the murderer leave the room?"

"The door wasn't locked," I said. "The door was bolted from the inside."

"And the windows are barred. Exactly."

"Perhaps the murderer just melted through the wall."

My mother frowned. She's a small, bright-eyed woman with eyes like custard-apple seeds. Dark and polished. "Don't be silly, Mahamaya," she said. "You know more than you're saying."

She was right of course, but perhaps I should begin at the beginning. With my childhood.

I was nine and my brothers were eleven and thirteen when my mother left my father and returned to my grandfather's house. I remember there was something of a scandal (I don't believe that in their hearts my uncles have forgiven her yet) but my mother claimed that if my uncles were entitled to shelter in their father's house, so was she.

I think, in retrospect, my grandfather let her stay because he knew that if he didn't, she'd take a train to god knows where. And he liked us.

So, she was given two rooms just below the terrace, and we ate with the rest of the family. My mother taught science at a secondary school and we'd take the tram in together every morning.

It was an old house, my grandfather's house in Tollygunge and I would spend hours on the terrace, beneath a cloth awning doing my homework or just day-dreaming. Bright fields stretched beyond the back wall of the house, there was a canal that glinted in the sun and a clump of tall *tal* trees that my brothers claimed was haunted.

I remember it was a monsoon day when that yellow light stains the sky, and you feel with a quiver in the marrow of your bones the mystery of all creation, that I heard someone call my name. "Mahamaya, Mahamaya."

It was a girl's voice and I looked over the wall into the grounds next to ours. The Lahiri House. It was a majestic house, (whereas ours was shabby) with a portico and wide verandahs. I had often seen a polished black Bentley on the gravelled driveway, and I had longed to touch it.

That evening I did. And my friendship with the Lahiri children began.

Sharani was the youngest and she was my age. Phalguni was seven years older than us, and in between were their two brothers Tarun and Nikhil.

That was almost thirty years ago and all four children had returned home to be with their mother that Puja vacation, when she was murdered.

There were three others in the house that night as well Aloka, the maidservant, who looked after Ratnabali, Bimal, the cook, and Karuna Mashi, Ratnabali's younger sister.

No one had an alibi. The medical report had placed the time of death between 1.00 and 2.00 a.m. when everyone claimed that he or she had been asleep.

"But the room was bolted from the inside," my mother said. "How could that be?"

"It's simple," I said. "It's something we all knew as children. The bolt was a loose one, you see. All you had to do was shake the door gently from the other side, and the bolt would slip into place."

"Whoever killed her, knew that, and hoped, I suppose, to make it seem as though she'd died in her sleep. And anyway, Aloka says she never locked the room at night. In fact, Aloka says that she often slept with the door ajar, so that Aloka could hear her if she rang her bell."

I remembered that bell. It was a beautiful old brass bell, and it had been found on the window sill. The murderer must first have moved it there, so that Ratnabali's hand couldn't reach for it and ring it.

"No outsider," I said, "could have known about the bolt or the bell."

"You knew," my mother said.

"I didn't kill her!" I exclaimed. "What a thing to say."

"I'm sure you didn't," my mother said, "but you *are* an outsider."

"What does that mean?"

"It means, Mahamaya, that you should mind your own business. One of your childhood friends is a killer. So, yes, be there, if they need you. But don't ask too many questions."

"You don't think it's the servants or Karuna Mashi, then?"

"No," my mother said, "I don't. Why should they kill her? The Lahiri House was their home. They have nothing to gain."

The house was a large, spacious one with echoing rooms and shuttered windows that looked out onto a blue sky and the traceries of leaves. There were shadows everywhere and presiding over it all was Ratnabali.

To my nine year-old eyes she was the most beautiful woman I had ever seen. She had large watchful eyes, sombre and strong. And sometimes while we'd be playing hide-n-seek in the passage she might emerge as though from the shadows, a silent spectator of our antics.

I don't believe she ever approved of me and I didn't like her.

Yet, she never stopped me from playing with her children, eating with them or shrieking with pleasure in the sun of her back garden.

I loved that garden: its juxtaposition of roses, cannas and the green friendly nodding of banana leaves. It was a garden she had created and tended and the only thing that was forbidden us were the tamarinds off the tamarind tree.

I remember she had caught us once, eating tamarinds, Phalguni, Sharani and I.

"I thought I told you not to," she said. Her voice was low and she was shading her eyes against the sun. It was a hot summer's day, the temperature had hit 90° and I felt icy fingers walk up my spine.

Sharani began to wail and blubber that she was sorry. That she'd never eat another tamarind in her life.

"Of course you will," her mother said. "But only when I say you may. Is that clear, Sharani? Do you understand that?"

She said nothing to Phalguni. She just walked away. An hour later I discovered Phalguni behind the guava tree, a penknife at her wrist. I remember there were great red ants walking up the pale trunk and I whispered in horror, "What are you doing?"

She snapped the knife shut. "Nothing," she said. "Nothing."

She was as beautiful as her mother. But she was warm and vital. Like the blood pulsing in her veins. "You'd better go home now, Mahamaya," she said, her eyes smiling and strangely on fire.

I fled out of that garden, I remember. I returned with relief to the disorder of our rooms: shabby and comforting and the dry humour of my mother.

"What have you been doing?" my mother said. "Staring into the face of hell?"

"Yes," I said, "I have."

And yet, the next day, we played again in the back garden as though nothing had happened.

It's why I call it *The Tamarind Tree Murder*. Because in that incident lay the reason why it all happened. Why Ratnabali died as she did.

It had to do with forbidden things and an absence of faith.

Tollygunge had changed in the thirty years since I had first met the Lahiri children. The fields had become plots for co-operative housing societies; crude rectangular structures with gaggles of T.V. antennae.

These now overlooked the back garden of the Lahiri House where the rose garden had given way to a vegetable patch.

In that time too we had grown, married and left Calcutta, all of us. And yet, this year, by a strange coincidence, all four of the Lahiris had returned to their mother's for the Pujas within a day of each other, and without their families who were to follow later.

A little as though some *deus ex machina* had arranged things this way.

Spared the grandchildren, I suppose.

Sharani was the most relieved about that. "Thank goodness the children weren't here," she said.

She'd telephoned and asked me to come and stay with them for a few days. "Do you mind, Mahamaya?" she said. "It's all so unpleasant the police, the reporters. The questions." Her voice trailed away and a faraway look crept into her eyes.

"Nikhil says Ma is at peace. He says he knows that. He put some cannas in her room last night. As though she were still alive."

Nikhil had been Ratnabali's favourite child. He'd become a criminal lawyer, she had wanted that and she'd followed his cases like a hawk. A beautiful, gliding hawk. Watchful and proud.

They were all there at dinner that night: Tarunda, Phalguni, Nikhil and Sharani, Ratnabali's brood.

In each of them I saw something of their mother, an imprint so strong that involuntarily I shivered a little. In Phalguni I saw Ratnabali's face, in Tarunda (warm and affable otherwise), her tenacity. In Nikhil, her grace like that of an actor: lithe and sinuous, like some creature that could metamorphose itself into anything. That harboured secrets and was, in the end, intangible. In Sharani I saw flashes of her charm: some imp-like quality of laughter that might have been, had she not stifled it. Preferring shadows to the insouciance of a bright stream of light.

"I'm so glad you've come, Mahamaya," Nikhil said. (At thirteen I had been a little in love with him. I had never known a boy so kind or so graceful. My brothers had seemed crude and untidy a dreadful contrast.)

The Tamarind Tree Murder 163

Nikhil had taken my adoration in his stride. He would pay me little attentions that gave me pleasure, but they were always restrained enough so that I might not misread him. I suspect that was what made him such a good lawyer: a combination of anticipation and fairness.

A sort of grace, I suppose.

Tarunda was playing patience at the card-table. "What do you think, Mahamaya?" he said looking up. "Should we or shouldn't we have the shraddha here?"

"I really don't know," I stammered.

"Of course, you don't." Phalguni said. "No one does. It's unprecedented in our families. A murdered mother."

"Phalguni!" her aunt said. "You've been drinking!"

Phalguni looked at her with distaste. "No," she said, "as a matter of fact I haven't. I just don't hide from the truth. As you do."

"Do you really believe some 'thief' killed her? I don't. So I lock my room at night."

"Very wise," Nikhil said. "I must remember to do that too."

"Can't we talk of something else?" Sharani protested. "I mean Mahamaya's here now," she smiled wanly. "I thought that would make a difference."

I suppose for a while it did, but there was mistrust in the air. And concealed angers.

Over the next two days I began to pick up little bits of knowledge, inconsistencies, motives.

Phalguni and her husband, the manager of a tea estate in the Duars, were in financial trouble and they had asked Ratnabali for a loan which she'd apparently said "Yes" to.

"Dada doesn't believe her," Sharani said. I wasn't surprised. Tarunda was angry about the will (Ratnabali had divided everything equally among her four children: the property and all her other assets.)

Nikhil thought it was fair but Tarunda, a businessman, I suppose had had other plans! And Phalguni had said a strange thing one afternoon. She said the day she and Tarunda had arrived, they arrived before the others, she'd seen Tarunda rifling through their mother's desk.

He had made some excuse or other about a pen and writing-paper but Phalguni claimed he had seemed afraid.

And I knew, even as she said it, that *fear* lay behind the motive for the murder.

And then there was Sharani's claim that the night their mother had died she had knocked on Nikhil's door but no one had answered.

"Did you tell the police?" I said.

"No," she said, "I don't know what time it was. I woke up. I was feeling restless and so I thought I'd go and talk to him. Like I used to do as a child.

"He reads so late, so I thought he might be awake. I didn't look at my watch. But no one answered when I knocked on his door. And he's a light sleeper, you know."

"Why didn't you tell the police?"

"I couldn't," she said. "And anyway it doesn't mean anything."

"No," I said, "I suppose it doesn't."

Only, it also meant that Sharani too hadn't been in

her room at some point she knew what I was thinking, and she smiled sadly.

"Yes," she said, "any one of us could have done it. But I didn't kill her, Mahamaya. I could never have done that. Do you believe me?"

"Yes," I said, "I do."

I loved Sharani. I had to believe it.

That night I decided to go into Ratnabali's room. I had a sense that it held the secret. Something that the night would yield up to me.

The great four-poster bed had been made up as though she were still alive. The shadows of the bars fell on the floor. On the dressing-table the cannas drooped a little.

And then I saw him. Out in the garden downstairs. He was standing in the shadows, smoking.

And in that instant I recalled a childhood incident.

It had been a bright summer morning with a cacophony of birds in the trees. I had come running round the corner of the house and there in a great streak of sunlight I had seen him poised with a catapult, the stone zinging through the air and crashing into a pane of glass. A window in the house next door had cracked.

"Damn," I heard him cry as he flung the catapult to the ground. Nikhil turned and smiled at me ruefully, his eyes like amber in the sun. "I meant to hit the guava tree," he said. "There's a crow I don't like on it. Old Sinha-Roy's going to be furious. Isn't he, Mahamaya?"

I nodded. "What are you going to do?"

"Pay him for the pane, I suppose."

I was wide-eyed and eleven then and he was thirteen. "Do you have the money?" I whispered.

"Yes," he said. He was already quite beautiful. Ratnabali's favourite son. "Buried in a tin under the tamarind tree. Help me dig it up, Mahamaya."

We crouched there in the garden, the earth golden and russet in our fingers, like his eyes. Digging busily until with a muffled cry he brought it out. It was an old Player's cigarette tin with notes and coins inside.

"What a strange place to keep your money," I said.

"Isn't it?" he laughed. "But the tamarind tree's brought me luck, you see. No one will steal it, Mahamaya. Will you come with me?"

"Yes," I said, "of course." I'd have followed him anywhere. He was like a lake, Nikhil. The expressions skimming across his face like ripples. So open, and yet, somehow, elusive.

As though he wasn't quite there.

We were crossing the porch when we heard Ratnabali's voice. "Nikhil," she called. She was standing by the windows of the sitting room that overlooked the garden, a piece of intricate embroidery in her hands.

"Come inside," she said. "I want to talk to you."

It was cool inside that elegant, high-ceilinged room, and involuntarily I shivered. We had just come out of the sun.

"Mr. Sinha-Roy just telephoned," she said, her voice mellifluous, like honey. A dark and sombre honey. "He said you've just broken a window of his. With a catapult."

"I told him, of course, that he was mistaken. I said, 'I have told my son never to play with a catapult. Nikhil would not disobey his mother.' That *is* so, isn't it, Nikhil?"

I looked at him. I had seen chameleons in the garden petrified like this by a cat.

"Well," she said, "I was right to have said that, wasn't I, Nikhil?"

I looked out at the green and sunlit frenzy of the banana trees in the garden. "Yes," I heard him say, "you were right."

That day too I ran home helter-skelter to my mother. She looked up from the books she was correcting. "Where have you been?" she said.

"At the Lahiris."

"You're a little in awe of them, aren't you, Mahamaya?"

"Yes," I shrugged my shoulders. "I suppose so."

"You mustn't be," she said. "They're only human. Like the rest of us."

I hugged her then and looked with thankfulness into the warm, bright wisdom of her button eyes. My brave and laughing mother.

I looked around me again at Ratnabali's room, its niches and its shadows. Yes, yes, yes, I thought. It was in this, that the motive had lain. In her absence of laughter: in her disdain of all human folly and temptation.

She had despised failure and human weakness. The cannas were dead. And someone had murdered her.

I slipped out of the room, shutting the door behind me. And then I saw it. A light in the dining-room.

I ran down the stairs as quietly as I could: a voice inside me urging me to return to my room, another, like some hounded creature, saying: Go on, Mahamaya. Push the door open and you'll know.

I reached the foot of the stairs when the blow struck me on the back of my head and I blacked out.

When I regained consciousness the sunlight was streaming into the room and Sharani was standing beside me, a cup of tea in her hands.

"How are you feeling?" she said.

"Terrible. My head's splitting. Where am I?"

"In my room."

And then she told me. They had found him in the morning, hanging from the ceiling fan in the dining-room. A note left on the table.

"And he was Ma's favourite son," Sharani was crying. "And my favourite brother. You liked him too, didn't you?"

"Yes," I said, "I did." I had liked Nikhil very much.

It was in the newspapers that morning. News of Nikhil's bigamy. Apparently he had married a woman many years ago. She had run away with another man and he had never tried to find her.

There was a picture of the woman, hiding her face from the photographers. In a small town in Madhya Pradesh. She had tried to deny the story: she had another husband now and children.

"Poor soul," I said. "What will she do now?"

"I don't know," Sharani said. "Didi's going to write to her. He killed Ma because he didn't want Ma to find out. He knew they were going to break the story one of these days. He was a fool."

"Who was behind this?"

"I don't know," Sharani said. "I don't want to know. Nikhil had enemies in Delhi. It could have been anyone."

Many days later I read Nikhil's suicide note. "I killed Ma," it said. 'It was better this way. She is at rest. I suffer.

"I learnt that they were after the story, the day I left Delhi. I knew they'd get to us, sooner or later."

"Ma is spared this. The ignominy. Forgive me, if you can."

"Poor souls," my mother said. "Ratnabali and her son. They were alike, you know."

"Were they?"

"Yes," she said. 'They cared too much for perfection. I did too once. But then I grew to learn that we were all guilty of crimes: little ones, some witting, some unwitting. That absolute innocence is a myth.

"I'd watch the three of you. I loved you. But children never are what we would have them be. And so, I forgave myself. Do you understand?"

"Yes," I said, "I think I do."

"It was why I named you Mahamaya. My beautiful illusion."

We were on the terrace. It was early morning and the birds had begun to call.

I looked over into the garden of the Lahiri House. In a year it would be sold: the beautiful house Ratnabali had made the centre of her universe. But for a while anyway, cabbages and radishes would grow in the back garden. And the banana trees.

I saw Sharani come out, a shawl wrapped around her shoulders. She lifted her face to the sun. And I thought, yes, she is sad, but also, she is now free.

My gentle friend.

Sara

MANORAMA MATHAI

THERE ARE THOSE who flesh out the face of a wanted person, a criminal whom they have never seen, by linking disparate descriptions. So I have tried to fill in the personality of Sara from the hints dropped by people, those who have survived her but who remember her only in the light of what they consider was her wrongdoing; people who want to remember her only as an ordinary woman, one who casts no shadow on their past; those who want to conceal the real Sara.

Sometimes, especially as I wander through the old house where she lived, touching things that she touched, using objects that she used, I am confused. Is she me? Or was I Sara? Aren't all women one really? Those whose lives are lived in a small space, limited, forced to grow inwards, do not flash out in brilliance as individuals proud to stand out from the crowd.

It is strange, is it not, how the past can seep into the present and past happenings gain an importance that suggests there is an unseen kinship between them, between the dead and those who follow them. Perhaps this is because although the years have passed, nothing has changed significantly. I never knew Sara. She was my grandmother and I bear her name. From the fading photographs in my mother's album I can tell that I resemble her. Perhaps this accounts for my interest in a woman who died before I was born, a woman whose own daughter, my mother, barely remembers.

In a family like mine, however, the past is almost as real as the present, and the dead and gone never truly depart because they are always being recalled, more usually as exemplars of all that was good but sometimes, as in the case of Sara, as a warning of characteristics to avoid. Characteristics which are considered to be a recipe for disaster. So my mother, who never really knew Sara, will say to me, "You are just like your grandmother, she was headstrong like you and see where that ended. . ." and always these remarks tail off into a sigh.

My mother's cousin proudly displays a gold pendant she often wears, made, she always tells us proudly, from five gold sovereigns. This is the cue for a rush of nostalgia in which she recalls an incident from her infancy which she knows only by hearsay but which she tells with the relish of one who remembers:

"It was," she begins, settling herself comfortably with one or other child in her lap, her chewing tobacco near at hand, "after Aunt Sara had been taken back by her husband. Before she left for her husband's home (which was some thirty miles distant and a long journey by bullock-cart in those days) she came to see my mother, her younger sister. I had just been born and my aunt presented me with five gold sovereigns. That was the last time my mother saw her beloved elder sister."

We children had heard this story several times before, as indeed we had most of the family stories, but everyone knows that the old familiar tales, where you know exactly what is going to happen next, are the very best.

My aunt always sighed gustily at the end of this story as she held up the heavy gold ornament for us to admire. It occurred to me that whenever Sara was mentioned everybody sighed. Perhaps this was what whetted my curiosity about this ancestress of mine, whose picture posed her standing stiffly a little behind her husband who was seated in an elaborately carved chair, dressed in the European fashion of his time, frock-coated with a large watch chained around his stomach. Sara stands rigidly to attention and her large dark eyes stare out of the yellowing sepia with a luminosity that owes nothing to a long dead photographer's art.

Sara must have been about fifteen years old then. Nobody is very exact about age because when she and her sister were born nobody bothered to document the births. According to those who tell the story, Sara was about fifteen when she was married which, they say, was a very advanced age for a girl in those days. Perhaps Sara's marriage was delayed because she had a stepmother who was not inclined to bestir herself for a stepdaughter, and marriage-making is always women's work.

My mother smiles as she tells how all the women of her father's family were openly contemptuous of such an "old" bride but, she hastens to add, Sara was a barrister's daughter from a very distinguished family and therefore, despite the grumbling of the women, totally acceptable; besides, she was exceptionally fair-skinned and her nose, quite aquiline.

Sara's bridegroom was a medical student and a few short months after their wedding he departed to England to gain his MBBS. In those days people did not travel as frequently or as easily as they now do and there was no question of his bride accompanying him. She was left behind with his family for his mother to mould to their ways. Sara was the anchor, keeping her husband safe from temptation and consequent disaster while he sojourned in a strange land. His mother wanted no white daughter-in-law brought back by her son.

From what I remember of my grandfather the leave-taking between him and Sara must, I imagine, have been stiff and formal because that was the kind of man he was. I can imagine also how for the next few weeks his mother and sisters looked eagerly at Sara for signs of pregnancy. I have seen that eager probing look in my husband's mother's eyes and the cold hostility that has replaced it, so I think I know how they must have spied on Sara to discover any bouts of morning sickness or any unexplained longings for unusual food.

Sara did not conceive and her mother-in-law, like mine, was disappointed. I think I have warned you that Sara's story is often mine and so you must not mind that I sometimes step out of my role as a sort of narrator and speak of myself. With her son far away in a strange land for five years, Sara's mother-in-law's hopes of a grandchild receded and this made her impatient and sharp with Sara. Perhaps, too, the expression in Sara's dark eyes dismayed her and caused harsh words to rise to her lips. Perhaps other factors played their part in the dislike that grew between the two women.

Sara's stepmother had allowed the bride to be decked in gold as befitted the eldest daughter of a wealthy house, but as soon as the time came for the bride to depart to her new home, so the story goes, the stepmother relieved her of all but a few pieces. She took back the heavy gold earrings that pierced the entire ear, dragging down the lobes to make them hang fashionably low; thick bangles, ornate chains and a solid gold belt studded with rubies from Burma all failed to accompany Sara to her new home. This denudation of jewellery that should rightfully have gone with Sara could not have improved her mother-in-law's temper, and it was to be exacerbated by Sara's habit of escaping from the kitchen to disappear for unexplained lengths of time. It must have been quickly and painfully obvious to everyone in the house that the mother-in-law was finding it difficult to mould the daughter-in-law at all.

Sara's sisters-in-law often tell of the battles that raged between their mother and Sara. Though they never condone what they describe as Sara's headstrong behaviour, it is obvious that they unconsciously admired her for her ability to stand up to their martinet of a mother. Now old women, they have lost none of their respect, bordering on fear, of the little dried-up old woman who right up to the day she died held herself as straight as a ramrod. This description of my great-grandmother is based partly on my childhood memory of her, partly on the photographs that hang high up on the walls of the ancestral house.

Those photographs also show my great-grandfather who, according to the family chroniclers, was an impractical man always investing time and money in grandiose schemes that always fell through; he was hot-headed and, his daughters say, given to raging like a mad bull. These same chroniclers recount with relish how he could be stopped in his tracks by his tiny wife who had only to call out from an inner room: "Be quiet, from there." Her husband would immediately subside, spluttering meekly. Wives in those days did not call their husbands by their names and "from there" is the closest English translation I can manage for what my great-grandmother called her husband.

This is not my great-grandmother's story but it seems to me that there had been a hint of tragedy about her too. She had been married before and it seemed that she loved her young husband deeply, so much so that when her effects were turned out after her death, an old and faded picture of him was found. He had died quite soon after their marriage and as there were no children she had been remarried. She always maintained an outward show of great respect for her second husband but it is extremely doubtful that she ever loved him. The only thing that she has ever said on the subject was to her favourite grandchild, my mother, "My first husband was very unlike your grandfather," she told her, "my first husband was a gentle soul who loved books. He was always soft-spoken." Then, as my mother tells it, there would come a customary roar from her second husband as he argued with some friend or neighbour, and over her grandmother's face would appear an expression that she could never define.

Sara had good practice in standing up to unjust authority in her own girlhood home. Her father, the barrister, was a kindly man and a loving parent but he was, above all, a man who cherished peace in the home; the result was that, respected though he was as a purveyor of justice in court, there was little or no justice in his house. Sara's mother had died soon after her youngest child was born and in seeking a new mother for his three young children, he chose a widow who already had daughters of her own; it soon became apparent that she had no place in her heart for another woman's children.

This second wife was a woman of strong character who made sure that if she was crossed in any way her husband should not rest till she had been appeased. In her frequent confrontations with Sara the reverberations were such that the master of the house was reduced to begging his daughter to give in. It is from Sara's younger sister, Anna, that we have these accounts and her spirit was so thoroughly broken by the stepmother that she remained timid and afraid to the end of her days. It fell to Sara and their brother, Baben, to defend Anna and to divert the stepmother's attention away from her to themselves.

It is hard to believe that in a wealthy household, as my great-grandfather's was, one of the cruelties perpetrated against the children was to deprive them of food; it must be remembered, however, that the kitchen was the only domain where the woman was supreme and food was the most potent weapon to hand. So the stepmother made the stepdaughters perform all the menial tasks she could lay upon them and then she would deprive them of food, locking away in the larder all the delicacies of fish and meat, and the sweets prepared for her own children. By making Sara and Anna serve the rest of the family at meal times and eat only after they had all finished, she ensured that often enough there was little or nothing left for them --- they had to make do with the gravy after all the fish or meat had been eaten, and sometimes there was only rice porridge and a little salt fish left.

She did not dare do this to her stepson who ate with his father but, one day, as Aunt Anna tells it, "He came upon us eating plain rice and pickle and he began to question us because he had just eaten two kinds of fish and meat and vegetables. When Sara told him that often enough this was the only food we got he flew into a towering rage and entering the kitchen (something the men of the house never did) he threw all the pots and pans on the floor." Here Aunt Anna's eyes always opened wide as if she was once again re-living the horror and fascination of that event. "He made our stepmother open the store cupboards and then he stood over us till we had eaten our fill of everything he could find." This is my aunt's favourite story, and sometimes when I watch her pick fastidiously at her food and find fault with her daughter-in-law's cooking it occurs to me that perhaps she has never enjoyed a meal more than that one so long ago.

Obviously Baben could not always make sure that his sisters were properly fed and it fell to Sara to look after herself and Anna. She became an expert at picking locks and she took pleasure in defying the stepmother in every way she could, as often as not to deflect that lady's temper away from Anna to herself. One person who has survived from that time is Kurumba, the untouchable, who worked for the family and between whom and Sara there seems to have existed a bond that was never really broken. Kurumba came to the family as a little girl and soon enough became Sara's devoted slave. As an untouchable she was accustomed to degradation and careless cruelty; it was a revelation for her to see the highborn Sara treated not dissimilarly. It was Kurumba who accompanied Sara to her married home and I have often tried to get her to tell me what really happened there but she, like most old people, is happy enough to ramble on about the past till I get to a certain point in my questioning. Then her eyes film over and she says fretfully that she does not remember; sometimes she claims not to have been there during the crucial time, having returned to her own village.

From Kurumba's accounts it is clear that in her husband's home Sara was not starved of food, but it is obvious that she received no tenderness from her mother-in-law and must have perceived her as an enemy not altogether unlike the stepmother she had left behind. Perhaps this was inevitable. Daughters-in-law who had been cruelly treated when they were young seemed automatically to turn into harsh mothers-in-law when it came to their turn and so a vicious circle is formed of repression, physical cruelty and, at best, dislike.

Sara's only method of escape from the tyranny of her husband's mother was, literally, to escape from the house and into books. When I question Kurumba about that she says, "What do I know of books and reading? All I know is that she would get hold of some book or other, from where I do not know, then hide in different places and read. Her mother-in-law and sister-in-law would call her for hours and she would pretend not to hear. I always knew where she was but I never told them."

Sara loved to read, and insofar as he was able her father had encouraged this, buying her books from time to time. According to Anna she had read all the classics. Before the advent of her stepmother Sara had been sent by her liberal father to a school for girls run by two English missionaries, though, as Anna points out with a mixture of pride and censoriousness, it was not then the fashion to educate girls.

Sara's passion for books was, of course, anathema to her orthodox mother-in-law, especially since it was not the Bible that she read so religiously, and so it became necessary for her to hide while she read. She spent unconscionably long hours in the privy which stood at some distance from the house, or she lay curled up in the *thattumbara*, the attic, the rickety stairs of which she knew her mother-in-law would hesitate to negotiate.

I, too, have spent hours up in that old attic with its long sloping roof and low raftered ceiling; filled with the redundancies of the house below, it contained trunks filled with old papers and some with clothes, bell-metal lamps and pots and pans awaiting repair, antique carved furniture that had lost a leg or an arm, and the shapes and shadows all these made never ceased to fascinate me, though at first I went up there only to conceal myself in a game of hide and seek because I knew the other girls would be too scared to look for me in its dark recesses. It was later that I found the mat spread close to the skylight, and I can imagine how Sara lay curled up on it reading her purloined literature, which helped her perhaps to escape the realities of her life. I should know, I do it all the time, losing myself in the lives of other women as far removed from me as they can be. My mother-in-law often tells my husband that it is not normal for anyone to read as much as I do. Her words infer that I am wasting my time. . .

As a housebound daughter-in-law, strictly supervised, not free to come and go as she pleased, there was no way Sara could have got the books and magazines which she devoured in her secret hiding places. So where and how did she get hold of them? On some of my visits to that old house I have found magazines dating back to the years when Sara was young, and in one of the trunks up in the *thattumbara* there were several old books flung pell-mell, along with some letters on which the ink had faded so completely that it was unreadable ("Just as well," old Kurumba said tartly when I showed them to her, "old letters to other people are not for the young to read.")

Sara must have had somebody in that house, sympathetic to her, who brought her her books and magazines. In the village there is still only one bookshop and Sara could not have frequented it. Perhaps that was how a relationship began to develop between Sara and Verghese. I do not know, but I like to believe that Verghese, her husband's young cousin who lived in the house, was the one who supplied Sara with her reading material. Whatever its basis, no one at that time could accept a relationship between two young people of opposite sexes, and even less could anyone believe that such a relationship was not inherently sexual; after all, was that not the nature of men and women, what else did they have in common? My male cousins and I are never permitted to sit on a bed together and there is close supervision to prevent too much intimacy.

In a joint family there is little room for privacy and so it must soon have been perceived that Sara and Verghese were often in conversation together. Perhaps secret glances were intercepted, or intimate words overheard. What is far worse to my mind is that perhaps none of this occurred and that Sara never experienced the warmth that I know her nature must have craved.

Whatever the true nature of what took place that long time ago, all I know is what has come down the family grapevine with all its distortions and anxious attempts at a cover-up, probably to spare the feelings of Sara's descendants, one of whom at least would give anything to know the truth. But the trail is now hopelessly confused and the scent cold because there is no one now living who can and will tell me the truth. Not even old Kurumba who lived through it all and was perhaps the only person who genuinely loved Sara, because her memory travels selectively back and forth in the past, skirting the tragedy which she has entombed somewhere in the labyrinths of her mind.

So to me only a few bald facts are known and these have been woven into a fabric of family tales which have a quality almost of once upon a time; perhaps this is the only way one can come to terms with the tragedy of an erring ancestress and mitigate some of the pain and shame. Certainly, this pain and shame have created a veil that is hard to pierce. I speak of pain and shame to you and yet, the facts taken out of context to the time and the society in which they occurred, with no continuity with the months and weeks that led up to the catastrophe, may make it difficult for you to gauge the tragedy on the scale to which it belonged.

Sara loved to read, Sara was headstrong, Sara was careless about the cooking, Sara was unfaithful... can there be any connection between these things? Was she actually discovered in Verghese's arms? Nobody will say so and the elderly ladies who were young girls at the time, Sara's sisters-in-law, will say nothing. When I was young and unmarried such a topic was not considered fitting; now that I am married and really want to know the truth about the past, they say they cannot remember, that nobody told them anything.

We are back to the one bald fact that no one denies: Sara was thrown out of her husband's home and sent back in disgrace to her father's house. What happened to Verghese I do not know. My mother declares that she knows nothing about him and I am inclined to believe her, though I know full well that she would distort any fact if it did not suit her purpose. To her, as I suppose to all my family, respectability is above all else and adaptability, which means that if you are a woman you must give in to everybody and everything. The reason that I believe nothing is truly known about Verghese is because he was only a distant poor relation who had been brought to my grandfather's house as a gesture of generosity to a less well-off branch of the family. Among my people, you know, even a fourth cousin can lay a claim on you. But in this case, the scandal that ensued must have effectively cut any bonds that existed between the two families. Only old Kurumba sometimes says that he left the country and went to Malaya where, according to her, he became rich and owned rubber estates.

Eyewitnesses report that when Sara's palanquin reached her father's house he was reclining, as was his habit, on the verandah in his customary easy chair. Shading his eyes against the glare of the afternoon sun he saw his daughter descend from the palanquin and he rushed to embrace her. As he did so, however, the tears ran freely and he said, "Daughter, today you have rubbed coal on my face."

They say, and of course they hold it against her, that Sara was dry-eyed and that she offered no explanations.

What was said by his wife has not been recorded by posterity but I can well imagine her triumph at seeing her stepdaughter thus disgraced; after all, had she not always said that Sara was a bad lot and would bring disgrace on her poor father? Sometimes, as a young girl, I have visited that house where Sara's stepmother survived to a great old age. On these visits we were received by a benign fat old lady, a towel draped over her pendulous breasts (she had grown up at a time when only the lower classes covered their bosoms), who would welcome us with sweet smiles and loving embraces and I could never explain why my flesh shrank from that fat, moist body (she seemed to sweat so) or why I could not respond to her blandishments. But I believe it is because of my affinity with Sara. I was almost physically aware of her sufferings at this now benign old lady's hands.

My mother always said, "She is an old woman now and all that is in the past and has to be forgotten." She adds, "One cannot know or understand everything that has happened and it is not for us to judge our elders." But I do! I sit in judgement over all those who judged Sara. I sit in judgement over all those who set first Sara and now me adrift in a world without love, without the right to choose where we should and can love.

I tell you, my friend, I am like a leaky boat; no matter how much water is baled out there is always bitterness welling up, threatening to overflow and submerge me utterly. I ask myself: did Sara feel this way and are my feelings now but a bitter reflection of hers? The house in which she spent her bridal years always seemed to me to emanate a sadness, a forlornness of hope, which I as a child could feel, not comprehend, but which in the light of my own experience I have pieced together.

It was a dark house, its ceilings and walls of carved wood. The furniture was austere and the floor was a beautiful matt black that gave of no light, no gentle reflections. In the deep cool front verandah, shaded by creepers, beyond which lay the golden green blaze of banana and coconut palm and emerald paddy, only the men reclined in their easy chairs. It was the kitchen verandah where the women sat when they wanted light and air. And a young daughter-in-law was not expected to sit idle, always she must be busy, usually in the dark and smoky kitchen.

Sara was only in her teens when disgrace overtook her: she was childless, disgraced and as good as divorced, and that, I can tell you, was a fate worse than death in those days. I often try and imagine the years that followed for beautiful, high-spirited Sara and I can only believe that they must have been hellish.

You ask whether Sara had fallen in love with Verghese; I do not know and now will never know as the past daily recedes from me. If she loved him then the separation must have been cruel enough, but if there had been nothing between them except what suspecting minds and prurient eyes pieced together, how unjust must the punishment have seemed. Condemned to servitude by a triumphant stepmother, seeing the grief she had brought to a beloved father (his hair was said to have turned white overnight), unwanted by the husband she barely knew, with nothing to look forward to — I can imagine, can't you, how her spirit was gradually crushed.

Sara's sister Anna sometimes talked of this time, of how she often woke to hear her sister weeping in the night; but if in those midnight hours Sara confided anything to her young sister, then Anna has never revealed it. She herself never deviated from the straight and narrow, the path of duty, when her feet were set upon it. Married to an intellectual, she devoted herself to feeding his body and never impinged upon his mind. She could only condemn her sister's illicit relationship with a man other than her husband but because she was staunchly loyal, she never spoke of it until long after everybody concerned was dead, and even then it was only in generalizations.

So the years passed for Sara, spent in petty skirmishes with her stepmother and then even these seemed to have lost their fire for, as Anna told it, Sara no longer seemed to notice the skimpy food, seemed not to care about the taunts of stepmother and stepsisters. In their turn Baben and Anna got married and they left home, leaving Sara utterly alone. Her father greatly pitied her and, according to Kurumba, tried to do what he could to comfort her, but he was afraid to do too much for that brought down the wrath of his wife on both their heads.

I have a thin yellowing notebook which bears no name on its flyleaf but that I am certain belonged to Sara, and whose disjointed entries belong to this time. Some of the things she wrote in that notebook she also said to her sister for they have been repeated to us by her. "My life is running to waste like water that has been gathered in a leaky bucket," she wrote. "I have the appetite of a giant and I am given the diet of a pigmy." When Anna repeated this across the years I always felt that she thought her sister was referring to the meagre food doled out by the stepmother!

Unknown to Sara, negotiations were taking place between the two estranged families. Like most families in Kerala they were interconnected and had relations in common; one of these had taken it upon herself to bring about a reconciliation. At first Sara's husband's family remained adamant, they wanted no more of Sara. Then, apparently, they began to weaken and representatives went between the two families carrying suggestions and counter-suggestions.

I think this must have been the time that Sara's husband returned from England, a qualified doctor, ready to take up his place in the world. I would like to believe that he came back home and missed his beautiful young wife, that despite his humourlessness and pompous ways, in his heart he loved Sara and wanted her back. More likely, however, he realized that a divorcé (however innocent) would not necessarily be able to remarry advantageously. And my grandfather was a man who always weighed up the possible advantages of any action before taking it. Whatever the reason, he returned from England a qualified doctor, ready to set up practice and start a family. He agreed to take Sara back. Knowing my grandfather as I do, this taking back his wife was almost certainly as if she was to be on probation; my grandfather made his father-in-law understand clearly that any fall from grace meant Sara would be returned forthwith, without further hope of reprieve. So it was like a prisoner being let out on parole that Sara rejoined her husband, and she was redeemed almost at once by producing in the shortest possible time a son and heir; less than two years later my mother followed and perhaps they were a happy little family then.

I should like to think so, but when I look at the family album my heart sinks. In the photograph taken after my mother's birth Sara's eyes look into mine with what I can only call desperation. . . I have seen that look in my own mirror often enough. Sara holds my mother in her arms, while her son sits in his father's lap, but she looks away from them all. My grandfather's moustache is stiff, like everything else about him, he is carefully dressed, quite dapper, really, but there is no warmth there. You can see what I mean, can't you? Or do you think that I am imagining it all because I am unhappy? But see how Sara stands beside his seated figure, can you not see the space between them? It is a space which I believe was never bridged.

With some people the shadow of their death lays an aura about them; when they lose hope, they feel the core of their being draining away. I know. When one knows that one will never achieve the desire of one's heart and mind, one gives up. In Sara's eyes I see my own self-knowledge, I recognize my failure. I study these old family pictures often, there is one of my parents in which I see the beginnings of what is now my mother's constant exasperation and there is, there too, a separate yearning about them. My father is an agriculturist who would prefer to be a writer. His poems appear in magazines which never pay and while he "scribbles" (my mother's word) the land is neglected. Ours is a materialistic society (any spirituality there is manages to co-exist very comfortably) and my father is not one of its successes. My mother who should have married someone like her father, successful, correct, professional, is yoked instead to this hopeless romantic who values his books above his other possessions.

The women in our family are all mismatched and when it came to my turn my mother made sure that I should have what she wanted for herself. So here I am, married to a dentist, professionally qualified, dull, who spends his days peering into the mouth of decay. He is a very good dentist, it is no fault of his that there is no more, no fault of his that I need more. Would you say that it is my fault then? My fault, as it was Sara's? My mother says that I am a "romantic child with foolish notions" and she points out my husband is successful and growing richer every day, that all those who bare their teeth to him sing his praises. Of course, those are not quite her words, but I can interpret her satisfaction at my well-equipped house and well-stocked jewellery box.

To my mother-in-law it seems I have no rights because my body has failed in its primary duty, that of bringing forth a son and heir. Even a girl child would by this time be welcome, proving that there was hope. At first she used to concoct little potions for me, make me eat sesame seeds... to purify my blood, she said. My body's blood beats a rhythm which used to be a song but is now a lament. Sometimes I lie alone in my bed while my husband sits in his surgery making gold teeth for his patients. So it's more money for us and a proud possession for the patients and I wait my life away; like Sara's, my life too is running to waste like a tap left running; it irrigates no land and no garden blooms.

When my body cries out to his soundlessly: Wait! he does not hear and I am left abandoned, marooned, and only my pride keeps me afloat. Is this, then, what Sara knew? One can never know, then as now, for no woman talks of sex, it is not important to a decent woman, only motherhood is.

Some years after my mother was born Sara had another child, another son, and a few short months later she was dead. Once again the whole business is clouded in mystery, once again the family censorship comes into play. My mother believes the official version of the story: that Sara was nursing the new baby when he bit her nipple. The wound turned septic and Sara died of blood poisoning. In those days there were no antibiotics and certainly, in wealthy and influential families, no post-mortems.

This story, despite the psychological effect it might have had on the innocent perpetrator, was the story that the family clung to. Inevitably, however, there were whispers, the servants talked and the village gossips hinted darkly of suicide. Old Kurumba sometimes says, "She was not happy, is it any wonder that she did not live. One must fight for life if one wants it." Is this her way of saying that Sara took her own life? She will never be pressed into such an admission.

Well, Sara is almost forgotten now. Less than a year after her death my grandfather remarried and his second wife was a complete success. She was neither fair-skinned nor beautiful but they say my grandfather and his mother had had their fill of beauty and now wanted only a practical woman of good sense. As the village women say, a plain woman is more likely to tend to her duties than a beautiful one.

The second wife long survived her husband and though she has had her own share of sadness, she has never in the least aroused my interest. A practical woman, a sensible wife and mother, an adequate stepmother, nobody had a word to say against her and she filled all the space that poor Sara had left vacant.

You never saw in this second wife's eyes the expression I see in Sara's, an expression which even cardboard, yellowing with age, cannot conceal. There is a wild, a hungry look there. What was Sara seeking that she never found? I liken her to the canary about whom she used to tell stories to her younger sister. It was a pretty bird, one that lived in a gilded cage, expected to sing all day in blissful contentment. But sometimes this little bird went wild and beat its wings against its cage trying to fly out and upwards, only to fall to the floor. But, asked Sara, if we opened this cage what would the canary do? A bird bred in captivity cannot soar into the trackless blue sky; it cannot defend itself against the vultures that circle overhead; it cannot escape the prowling feral cat, nor the cruel child that would pull its feathers. Yet, if we set this little bird free, helpless as it is, perhaps it would find another like itself and sit in a mango tree and sing all day long whether anyone heard it or not.

Perhaps I have misrepresented Sara but I have not tried to deceive you; in my unhappiness I have tried to draw analogies, I have tried to describe passion, but I have only been able to rake over cold embers. I have tried to tell of a life lived in limbo, a soul in purgatory, but perhaps I was only telling of myself and did not, as I fancied, step through the mirror. An unreal life, not only because it is past, but because I have never known what love is, what it might be. There are no sensual scenes, no talk of beds and bosoms, no heaving guilt, no violence of passion, no shuddering orgasms. What I speak of in lowered tones for none but you to hear, is quiet desperation, silent festering.

More than half a century has passed and times have changed. Man has walked on the moon and women have babies without husbands and there is talk of women's rights. Why, they say even animals have rights these days. But some things never change. The tragedy of a woman caught between her duty to her society and family and her own deeper longings remains unchanged, in my world, at any rate, as in Sara's.

Notes on Authors

URMILA BANERJEE (b.1952) was educated in Calcutta and at Wellesley College in the United States. She lives in Bombay where she has been an English teacher for several years. Her stories have appeared in *The Bombay Literary Review*, *London Magazine* and *Chicago Review*. She is currently compiling a selection of stories for publication.

ACHLA BANSAL (b.1946) was brought up in Delhi. In 1980 she started writing short stories which have been published in various magazines and national dailies. Her first collection of short stories, *Once a Year it is March*, appeared in 1991, and a second is ready for publication. Her work has won acclaim and been translated into different Indian languages.

DEEP BEDI (b.1936) was educated in Kanpur and Hyderabad. The eldest of four children, she began writing while at college, and initially wrote only in Hindi. Her English writing began in 1976 when she returned to India after an eight-year spell in Beirut with her husband. A mother of three children, Deep Bedi is now a Buddhist and lives in Bangalore where she continues to write.

RITU BHATIA (b.1962) is a microbiologist who turned from the laboratory to writing on health and nutrition for newspapers and magazines. In 1987 she began writing short stories, some of which have been published in Indian journals.

SHAMA FUTEHALLY (b.1952) studied English at the universities of Bombay and Leeds. She was a lecturer in English at Bombay University for six years; and in Cultural History at the School of Architecture, Ahmedabad, for two years. Her reviews, articles and short stories have appeared in Indian journals. She is currently living in New Delhi, translating the poems of Mirabai, and working on her fiction.

GITHA HARIHARAN (b.1954) was educated in Bombay, Manila, and in the United States. Since 1979 she has worked in publishing, first as an editor in a large publishing house, and subsequently as a freelancer. Several of her short stories have been published in magazines and journals. Her first novel, *The Thousand Faces of Night*, will be published in mid-1992 by Penguin (India). A collection of stories entitled *The Art of Dying and Other Stories*, is also forthcoming from Penguin.

VISHWAPRIYA L. IYENGAR (b.1958) was educated in Bangalore, and has worked as a journalist in New Delhi and Bangalore. As a social activist, she has written film-scripts on fisherfolk, child labour, street children and stone quarry workers, and on sundry environmental issues. Her short stories have been widely published in India and abroad.

Notes on Authors

MANJU KAK (b.1952) was educated in Lucknow, and has been a teacher of history, a broadcaster, painter, writer and compere. She has worked as a consultant with the Hongkong Polytechnic, taught at the Open Learning Institute in Hongkong, contributed features to newspapers and magazines, and held exhibitions of her oil and water-colour paintings. Her short stories have won awards, and she is currently working as a free-lance feature writer in Delhi.

MANORAMA MATHAI (b.1936) was educated at Delhi and Oxford universities. She has worked for UNICEF and CARE, and also as a free-lance writer and film-maker in many countries. An earlier collection of her stories, *Lilies that Fester*, was published by the Writers Workshop in 1988; a new novel, *Mulligatawny Soup*, is forthcoming from Penguin (India).

RUCHIRA MUKERJEE (b.1951) was educated in Lucknow and spent her early life in Uttar Pradesh. She studied English literature and taught briefly at Allahabad University before joining the civil services. Her first publications, while she taught, were poems; her short stories have appeared in *Imprint*, and she has just completed her first novel.

MANJULA PADMANABHAN (b.1953) is a cartoonist and writer, currently living in New Delhi. She has worked as a free-lance illustrator for a number of leading newspapers and magazines, and has illustrated 21 books for children. She has written two plays, of which the first, *Lights Out*, was performed in Bombay in 1986. Her comic strip, SUKI, appears daily in *The Pioneer*.

SHALINI SARAN (b.1951) is a free-lance travel writer and photographer based in New Delhi. Her articles and photographs have appeared in travel magazines and in books published in India, Hongkong and Germany. She has recently begun writing short stories.

SUBHADRA SEN GUPTA (b.1952) was educated mostly in Delhi. She has been writing since her days at university and has published stories for children, as well as a comic strip. She has recently completed two collections of stories, one for children and one for adults, both to be published shortly. She currently works in advertising as a copywriter.

BULBUL SHARMA (b.1952) was educated in Madhya Pradesh and at Jawaharlal Nehru University, Delhi, following which she studied Russian literature in Moscow. A well-known painter and print-maker, she has had several solo and group exhibitions of her work; she also regularly conducts nature and art workshops for Jagriti, an organisation working with street children in Delhi. A keen bird-watcher, Bulbul has written a book on Indian birds (1991), and one on Indian trees (forthcoming). She is also the author of a book of stories, *My Sainted Aunts* (1992).